MW01596089

East O' the Sun and West O' the Moon and other Norwegian Folk Tales

by

Gudrun Thorne-Thomsen

The Echo Library 2006

Published by

The Echo Library

Echo Library
131 High St.
Teddington
Middlesex TW11 8HH

www.echo-library.com

Please report serious faults in the text to complaints@echo-library.com

ISBN 1-40681-172-6

FOREWORD

In recent years there has been a wholesome revival of the ancient art of story-telling. The most thoughtful, progressive educators have come to recognize the culture value of folk and fairy stories, fables and legends, not only as means of fostering and directing the power of the child's imagination, but as a basis for literary interpretation and appreciation throughout life.

This condition has given rise to a demand for the best material in each of these several lines. Some editors have gleaned from one field; some from several. It is the aim of this little book to bring together only the very best from the rich stores of Norwegian folk-lore. All these stories have been told many times by the editor to varied audiences of children and to those who are "older grown." Each has proved its power to make the universal appeal.

In preparing the stories for publication, the aim has been to preserve, as much as possible, in vocabulary and idiom, the original folk-lore language, and to retain the conversational style of the teller of tales, in order that the sympathetic young reader may, in greater or less degree, be translated into the atmosphere of the old-time story-hour.

GUDRUN THORNE-THOMSEN.

4

CONTENTS

EAST O' THE SUN AND WEST O' THE MOON

Once on a time there was a poor woodcutter who had so many children that he had not much of either food or clothing to give them. Pretty children they all were, but the prettiest was the youngest daughter, who was so lovely there was no end to her loveliness.

It was on a Thursday evening late in the fall of the year. The weather was wild and rough outside, and it was cruelly dark. The rain fell and the wind blew till the walls of the cottage shook. There they all sat round the fire busy with this thing and that. Just then, all at once, something gave three taps at the window pane. Then the father went out to see what was the matter, and, when he got out of doors, what should he see but a great White Bear.

"Good evening to you!" said the White Bear.

"The same to you," said the man.

"Will you give me your youngest daughter? If you will, I'll make you as rich as you are now poor," said the Bear.

Well, the man would not be at all sorry to be so rich;—but give him his prettiest lassie, no, that he couldn't do, so he said "No" outright and closed the door both tight and well. But the Bear called out, "I'll give you time to think; next Thursday night I'll come for your answer."

Now, the lassie had heard every word that the Bear had said, and before the next Thursday evening came, she had washed and mended her rags, made herself as neat as she could, and was ready to start. I can't say her packing gave her much trouble.

Next Thursday evening came the White Bear to fetch her, and she got upon his back with her bundle, and off they went. So when they had gone a bit of the way, the White Bear said, "Are you afraid?"

"No, not at all," said the lassie.

"Well! mind and hold tight by my shaggy coat, and then there's nothing to fear," added the Bear.

So she rode a long, long way, till they came to a great steep hill. There on the face of it the White Bear gave a knock, and a door opened, and they came into a castle, where there were many rooms all lit up, gleaming with silver and gold, and there too was a table ready laid, and it was all as grand as grand could be. Then the White Bear gave her a silver bell. When she wanted anything she had only to ring it, and she would get what she wanted at once.

Well, when she had had supper and evening wore on, she became sleepy because of her journey. She thought she would like to go to bed, so she rang the bell. She had scarce taken hold of it before she came into a chamber where there were two beds as fair and white as any one would wish to sleep in. But when she had put out the light and gone to bed some one came into the room and lay down in the other bed. Now this happened every night, but she never saw who it was, for he always came after she had put out the light; and, before the day dawned, he was up and off again.

So things went on for a while, the lassie having everything she wanted. But you must know, that no human being did she see from morning till night, only the White Bear could she talk to, and she did not know what man or monster it might be who came to sleep in her room by night. At last she began to be silent and sorrowful and would neither eat nor drink.

One day the White Bear came to her and said: "Lassie, why are you so sorrowful? This castle and all that is in it are yours, the silver bell will give you anything that you wish. I only beg one thing of you—ask no questions, trust me and nothing shall harm you. So now be happy again." But still the lassie had no peace of mind, for one thing she wished to know: Who it was who came in the night and slept in her room? All day long and all night long she wondered and longed to know, and she fretted and pined away.

So one night, when she could not stand it any longer and she heard that he slept, she got up, lit a bit of a candle, and let the light shine on him. Then she saw that he was the loveliest Prince one ever set eyes on, and she bent over and kissed him. But, as she kissed him, she dropped three drops of hot tallow on his shirt, and he woke up.

"What have you done?" he cried; "now you have made us both unlucky, for had you held out only this one year, I had been freed. For I am the White Bear by day and a man by night. It is a wicked witch who has bewitched me; and now I must set off from you to her. She lives in a castle which stands East o' the Sun and West o' the Moon, and there are many trolls and witches there and one of those is the wife I must now have."

She wept, but there was no help for it; go he must.

Then she asked if she mightn't go with him?

No, she mightn't.

"Tell me the way then," she said, "and I'll search you out; that, surely, I may get leave to do."

"Yes, you may do that," he said, "but there is no way to that place. It lies East o' the Sun and West o' the Moon and thither you can never find your way." And at that very moment both Prince and castle were gone, and she lay on a little green patch in the midst of the gloomy thick wood, and by her side lay the same bundle of rags she had brought with her from home.

Then she wept and wept till she was tired, and all the while she thought of the lovely Prince and how she should find him.

So at last she set out on her way and walked many, many days and whomever she met she asked: "Can you tell me the way to the castle that lies East o' the Sun and West o' the Moon?" But no one could tell her.

And on she went a weary time. Both hungry and tired was she when she got to the East Wind's house one morning. There she asked the East Wind if he could tell her the way to the Prince who dwelt East o' the Sun and West o' the Moon. Yes, the East Wind had often heard tell of it, the Prince, and the castle, but he couldn't tell the way, for he had never blown so far.

"But, if you will, I'll go with you to my brother the West Wind. Maybe he knows, for he's much stronger. So, if you will just get on my back, I'll carry you thither."

Yes, she got on his back, and I can tell you they went briskly along.

So when they got there, they went into the West Wind's house, and the East Wind said that the lassie he had brought was the one who ought to marry the Prince who lived in the castle East o' the Sun and West o' the Moon; and that she had set out to seek him, and would be glad to know if the West Wind knew how to get to the castle.

"Nay," said the West Wind, "so far I've never blown; but if you will, I'll go with you to our brother the South Wind, for he is much stronger than either of us, and he has flapped his wings far and wide. Maybe he'll tell you. You can get on my back and I'll carry you to him."

Yes, she got on his back, and so they travelled to the South Wind, and were not long on the way, either.

When they got there, the West Wind asked him if he could tell her the way to the castle that lay East o' the Sun and West o' the Moon, for it was she who ought to marry the Prince who lived there.

"You don't say so. That's she, is it?" said the South Wind.

"Well, I have blustered about in most places in my time, but that far I have never blown; however, if you will, I'll take you to my brother the North Wind; he is the oldest and strongest of all of us, and if he doesn't know where it is, you'll never find anyone in the world to tell you. You can get on my back and I'll carry you thither."

Yes, she got on his back, and away he went from his house at a fine rate. And this time, too, she was not long on the way. When they got near the North Wind's house he was so wild and cross that cold puffs came from him.

"Heigh, there, what do you want?" he bawled out to them ever so far off, so that it struck them with an icy shiver.

"Well," said the South Wind, "you needn't be so put out, for here I am your brother, the South Wind, and here is the lassie who ought to marry the Prince who dwells in the castle that lies East o' the Sun and West o' the Moon. She wants to ask you, if you ever were there, and can tell her the way, for she would be so glad to find him again."

"Yes, I know well enough where it is," said the North Wind. "Once in my life I blew an aspen leaf thither, but I was so tired I couldn't blow a puff for ever so many days after it. But if you really wish to go thither, and aren't afraid to come along with me, I'll take you on my back and see if I can blow you there."

"Yes! and thank you," she said, for she must and would get thither if it were possible in any way; and as for fear, however madly he went, she wouldn't be at all afraid.

"Very well then," said the North Wind, "but you must sleep here to-night, for we must have the whole day before us if we're to get thither at all."

Early next morning the North Wind woke her, and puffed himself up, and blew himself out, and made himself so stout and big, it was gruesome to look at him. And so off she went, high on the back of the North Wind up through the air, as if they would never stop till they got to the world's end.

Down here below there was a terrible storm; it threw down long tracts of woodland and many houses, and when it swept over the great sea ships foundered by hundreds.

So they tore on and on,—no one can believe how far they went,—and all the while they still went over the sea, and the North Wind got more and more weary, and so out of breath he could scarce bring out a puff, and his wings drooped and drooped, till at last he sunk so low that the crests of the waves lashed over her heels.

"Are you afraid?" said the North Wind.

She wasn't.

But they were not very far from land; and the North Wind had still so much strength left in him that he managed to throw her up on shore close by the castle which lay East o' the Sun and West o' the Moon; but then he was so weak and worn out, that he had to stay there and rest many days before he could get home again.

And now the lassie began to look about her and to think of how she might free the Prince, but nowhere did she see a sign of life.

Then she sat herself down right under the castle windows, and as soon as the sun went down, out they came, trolls and witches, red-eyed, long-nosed, hunch-backed hags, tumbling over each other, scolding, hurrying and scurrying hither and thither.

At first they almost frightened the life out of her, but when she had watched them awhile and they had not noticed her, she took courage and walked up to one of them and said: "Pray tell me what goes on here to-night that you are all so busy, and could I perhaps get something to do for a night's lodging and a bit of food?"

"Ha, ha, ha!" laughed the horrid witch, "and where do you come from that you do not know that it is to-night that the Prince chooses his bride. When the moon stands high over the tree tops yonder we meet in the clearing by the old oak. There the caldrons are ready with boiling lye, for don't you know?—he's going to choose for his bride the one who can wash three spots of tallow from his shirt, Ha, ha, ha!"

And the wicked witch hurried off again, laughing such a horrible laugh that it made the lassie's blood run cold.

But now the trolls and witches came trooping out of the very earth, it seemed, and all turned their steps toward the clearing in the woods.

So the lassie went too, and found a place among the rest. Now the moon stood high above the tree tops, and there was the caldron in the middle and round about sat the trolls and witches;—such gruesome company I'm sure you were never in. Then came the Prince; he looked about from one to the other, and he saw the lassie, and his face grew white, but he said nothing.

"Now, let's begin," said a witch with a nose three ells long. She was sure she was going to have the Prince, and she began to wash away as hard as she could, but the more she rubbed and scrubbed, the bigger the spots grew.

"Ah!" said an old hag, "you can't wash, let me try."

But she hadn't long taken the shirt in hand, before it was far worse than ever, and with all her rubbing and scrubbing and wringing, the spots grew bigger and blacker, and the darker and uglier was the shirt.

Then all the other trolls began to wash, but the longer it lasted, the blacker and uglier the shirt grew, till at last it was as black all over as if it had been up the chimney.

"Ah!" said the Prince, "you're none of you worth a straw, you can't wash. Why there sits a beggar lassie, I'll be bound she knows how to wash better than the whole lot of you. Come here, lassie," he shouted.

"Can you wash the shirt clean, lassie?" said he.

"I don't know," she said, "but I think I can."

And almost before she had taken it and dipped it in the water, it was as white as snow, and whiter still.

"Yes; you are the lassie for me," said the Prince.

At that moment the sun rose and the whole pack of trolls turned to stone.

There you may see them to this very day sitting around in a circle, big ones and little ones, all hard, cold stone.

But the Prince took the lassie by the hand and they flitted away as far as they could from the castle that lay East o' the Sun and West o' the Moon.

THE THREE BILLY GOATS GRUFF

Once on a time there were three Billy Goats, who were to go up to the hillside to make themselves fat, and the family name of the goats was "Gruff."

On the way up was a bridge, over a river which they had to cross, and under the bridge lived a great ugly Troll with eyes as big as saucers, and a nose as long as a poker.

First of all came the youngest Billy Goat Gruff to cross the bridge. "Trip, trap; trip, trap!" went the bridge.

"*Who's that tripping over my bridge?*" roared the Troll.

"Oh, it is only I, the tiniest Billy Goat Gruff, and I'm going up to the hillside to make myself fat," said the Billy Goat, with such a small voice.

"Now, I'm coming to gobble you up," said the Troll.

"Oh, no! pray do not take me, I'm too little, that I am," said the Billy Goat; "wait a bit till the second Billy Goat Gruff comes, he's much bigger."

"Well! be off with you," said the Troll.

A little while after came the second Billy Goat Gruff across the bridge.

"Trip, trap! trip, trap! trip, trap!" went the bridge.

"*Who is that tripping over my bridge?*" roared the Troll.

"Oh, it's the second Billy Goat Gruff, and I'm going up to the hillside to make myself fat," said the Billy Goat. Nor had he such a small voice, either.

"Now, I'm coming to gobble you up!" said the Troll.

"Oh, no! don't take me, wait a little till the big Billy Goat comes, he's much bigger."

"Very well! be off with you," said the Troll.

But just then up came the big Billy Goat Gruff.

"Trip, trap! trip, trap! trip, trap!" went the bridge, for the Billy Goat was so heavy that the bridge creaked and groaned under him.

"*Who's that tramping on my bridge?*" roared the Troll.

"It's I! the big Billy Goat Gruff," said the Billy Goat, and he had a big hoarse voice.

"Now, I'm coming to gobble you up!" roared the troll.

"*Well come! I have two spears so stout,*
With them I'll thrust your eyeballs out;
I have besides two great big stones,
With them I'll crush you body and bones!"

That was what the big Billy Goat said; so he flew at the Troll, and thrust him with his horns, and crushed him to bits, body and bones, and tossed him out into the river, and after that he went up to the hillside.

There the Billy Goats got so fat that they were scarcely able to walk home again, and if they haven't grown thinner, why they're still fat; and so,—
"Snip, snap, stout.
This tale's told out."

TAPER TOM

Once on a time there was a King who had a daughter, and she was so lovely that her good looks were well known far and near. But she was so sad and serious she could never be got to laugh, and besides, she was so high and mighty that she said "No" to all who came to woo her. She would have none of them, were they ever so grand—lords or princes,—it was all the same.

The King had long ago become tired of this, for he thought she might just as well marry; she, too, like all other people. There was no use in waiting; she was quite old enough, nor would she be any richer, for she was to have half the kingdom,—that came to her as her mother's heir.

So he had word sent throughout the kingdom, that anyone who could get his daughter to laugh should have her for his wife and half the kingdom besides. But, if there was anyone who tried and could not, he was to have a sound thrashing. And sure it was that there were many sore backs in that kingdom, for lovers and wooers came from north and south, and east and west, thinking it nothing at all to make a King's daughter laugh. And gay fellows they were, some of them too, but for all their tricks and capers there sat the Princess, just as sad and serious as she had been before.

Now, not far from the palace lived a man who had three sons, and they, too, had heard how the King had given it out that the man who could make the Princess laugh was to have her to wife and half the kingdom.

The eldest was for setting off first. So he strode off, and when he came to the King's grange, he told the King he would be glad to try to make the Princess laugh.

"All very well, my man," said the King, "but it's sure to be of no use, for so many have been here and tried. My daughter is so sorrowful it's no use trying, and it's not my wish that anyone should come to grief."

But the lad thought he would like to try. It couldn't be such a very hard thing for him to get the Princess to laugh, for so many had laughed at him, both gentle and simple, when he enlisted for a soldier and was drilled by Corporal Jack.

So he went off to the courtyard, under the Princess's window, and began to go through his drill as Corporal Jack had taught him. But it was no good, the Princess was just as sad and serious and did not so much as smile at him once. So they took him and thrashed him well, and sent him home again.

Well, he had hardly got home before his second brother wanted to set off. He was a schoolmaster, and the funniest figure one ever laid eyes upon; he was lopsided, for he had one leg shorter than the other, and one moment he was as little as a boy, and in another, when he stood on his long leg, he was as tall and long as a Troll. Besides this he was a powerful preacher.

So when he came to the king's palace, and said he wished to make the Princess laugh, the King thought it might not be so unlikely after all. "But mercy on you," he said, "if you don't make her laugh. We are for laying it on harder and harder for every one that fails."

Then the schoolmaster strode off to the courtyard, and put himself before the Princess's window, and read and preached like seven parsons, and sang and chanted like seven clerks, as loud as all the parsons and clerks in the country round.

The King laughed loud at him, and the Princess almost smiled a little, but then became as sad and serious as ever, and so it fared no better with Paul, the schoolmaster, than with Peter the soldier—for you must know one was called Peter and the other Paul. So they took him and flogged him well, and then they sent him home again.

Then the youngest, whose name was Taper Tom, was all for setting out. But his brothers laughed and jeered at him, and showed him their sore backs, and his father said it was no use for him to go for he had no sense. Was it not true that he neither knew anything nor could do anything? There he sat in the hearth, like a cat, and grubbed in the ashes and split tapers. That was why they called him "Taper Tom." But Taper Tom would not give in, and so they got tired of his growling; and at last he, too, got leave to go to the king's palace to try his luck.

When he got there he did not say that he wished to try to make the Princess laugh, but asked if he could get work there. No, they had no place for him, but for all that Taper Tom would not give up. In such a big palace they must want someone to carry wood and water for the kitchen maid,—that was what he said. And the king thought it might very well be, for he, too, got tired of his teasing. In the end Taper Tom stayed there to carry wood and water for the kitchen maid.

So one day, when he was going to fetch water from the brook, he set eyes upon a big fish which lay under an old fir stump, where the water had eaten into the bank, and he put his bucket softly under the fish and caught it. But as he was gong home to the grange he met an old woman who led a golden goose by a string.

"Good-day, godmother," said Taper Tom, "that's a pretty bird you have, and what fine feathers! If one only had such feathers one might leave off splitting fir tapers."

The goody was just as pleased with the fish Tom had in his bucket and said, if he would give her the fish, he might have the golden goose. And it was such a curious goose. When any one touched it he stuck fast to it, if Tom only said, "If you want to come along, hang on." Of course, Taper Tom was willing enough to make the exchange. "A bird is as good as a fish any day," he said to himself, "and, if it's such a bird as you say, I can use it as a fish hook." That was what he said to the goody, and he was much pleased with the goose.

Now, he had not gone far before he met another old woman. As soon as she saw the lovely golden goose she spoke prettily, and coaxed and begged Tom to give her leave to stroke his lovely golden goose.

"With all my heart," said Taper Tom, and just as she stroked the goose he said, "If you want to come along, hang on."

The goody pulled and tore, but she was forced to hang on whether she would or not, and Taper Tom went on as though he alone were with the golden goose.

When he had gone a bit farther, he met a man who had had a quarrel with the old woman for a trick she had played him. So, when he saw how hard she struggled and strove to get free, and how fast she stuck, he thought he would just pay her off the old grudge, and so he gave her a kick with his foot.

"If you want to come along, hang on!" called out Tom, and then the old man had to hop along on one leg, whether he would or not. When he tore and tugged and tried to get loose—it was still worse for him, for he all but fell flat on his back every step he took.

In this way they went on a good bit till they had nearly reached the King's palace.

There they met the King's smith, who was going to the smithy, and had a great pair of tongs in his hand. Now you must know this smith was a merry fellow, full of both tricks and pranks, and when he saw this string come hobbling and limping along, he laughed so that he was almost bent double. Then he bawled out, "Surely this is a new flock of geese the Princess is going to have—Ah, here is the gander that toddles in front. Goosey! goosey! goosey!" he called, and with that he threw his hands about as though he were scattering corn for the geese.

But the flock never stopped—on it went and all that the goody and the man did was to look daggers at the smith for making fun of them. Then the smith went on:

"It would be fine fun to see if I could hold the whole flock, so many as they are," for he was a stout strong fellow. So he took hold with his big tongs by the old man's coat tail, and the man all the while screeched and wriggled. But Taper Tom only said:

"If you want to come along, hang on!" So the smith had to go along too. He bent his back and stuck his heels into the ground and tried to get loose, but it was all no good. He stuck fast, as though he had been screwed tight with his own vise, and whether he would or not, he had to dance along with the rest.

So, when they came near to the King's palace, the dog ran out and began to bark as though they were wolves and beggars. And when the Princess, looking out of the window to see what was the matter, set eyes on this strange pack, she laughed softly to herself. But Taper Tom was not content with that:

"Bide a bit," he said, "she will soon have to make a noise." And as he said that he turned off with his band to the back of the palace.

When they passed by the kitchen the door stood open, and the cook was just stirring the porridge. But when she saw Taper Tom and his pack she came running out at the door, with her broom in one hand and a ladle full of smoking porridge in the other, and she laughed as though her sides would split. And when she saw the smith there too, she bent double and went off again in a loud peal of laughter. But when she had had her laugh out, she too thought the golden goose so lovely she must just stroke it.

"Taper Tom! Taper Tom!" she called out, and came running out with the ladle of porridge in her fist, "Give me leave to pet that pretty bird of yours'?"

"Better come and pet me," said the smith. But when the cook heard that she got angry.

"What is that you say?" she cried and gave the smith a box on his ears with the ladle.

"If you want to come along, hang on," said Taper Tom. So she stuck fast too, and for all her kicks and plunges, and all her scolding and screaming, and all her riving and striving, she too had to limp along with them.

Soon the whole company came under the Princess's window. There she stood waiting for them. And when she saw they had taken the cook too, with her ladle and broom, she opened her mouth wide, and laughed so loud that the King had to hold her upright.

So Taper Tom got the Princess and half the kingdom, and they say he kept her in high spirits with his tricks and pranks till the end of her days.

WHY THE BEAR IS STUMPY-TAILED

One day the Bear met the Fox, who came slinking along with a string of fish he had stolen.

"Where did you get those?" asked the Bear.

"Oh! my Lord Bruin, I've been out fishing and caught them," said the Fox.

So the Bear had a mind to learn to fish too, and bade the Fox tell him how he was to set about it.

"Oh! it is an easy craft for you," answered the Fox, "and soon learned. You've only to go upon the ice, cut a hole, stick your tail down into it, and hold it there as long as you can. You're not to mind if your tail smarts a little; that's when the fish bite. The longer you hold it there the more fish you'll get; and then all at once out with it, with a cross pull sideways, and with a strong pull too."

Yes, the Bear did as the Fox had said, and held his tail a long, long time down in the hole, till it was frozen in fast. Then he pulled it out with a cross pull, and it snapped short off. That's why Bruin goes about with a stumpy tail to this very day.

REYNARD AND THE COCK

Once on a time there was a cock who stood on the barnyard fence and crowed and flapped his wings. Then the fox came by.

"Good-day," said Reynard. "I have heard you crowing so nicely, but can you stand on one leg and crow, and wink your eyes?"

"Oh, yes," said the cock, "I can do that very well." So he stood on one leg and crowed, but he winked only with one eye, and when he had done that he made himself big and flapped his wings, as though he had done a great thing.

"Very pretty, to be sure," said Reynard. "Almost as pretty as when the parson preaches in church, but can you stand on one leg and wink both your eyes at once? I hardly think you can."

"Can't I though!" said the cock, and stood on one leg, and winked both his eyes and crowed. But Reynard caught hold of him, took him by the throat, and threw him on his back, so that he was off to the wood before he had crowed his crow out, as fast as Reynard could lay legs to the ground.

When they had come under an old spruce fir, Reynard threw the cock on the ground, and set his paw on his breast, and was going to take a bite: "You are a heathen, Reynard!" said the cock. "Good Christians say grace before they eat."

But Reynard would be no heathen, no indeed. So he let go his hold, and was about to fold his paws over his breast, and say grace—but pop! up flew the cock into a tree.

"You shan't get off for all that," said Reynard to himself. So he went away, and came again with a few chips which the woodcutters had left. The cock peeped and peered to see what they could be.

"What is that you have there?" he asked.

"These are letters I have just got," said Reynard, "won't you help me to read them, for I don't know how to read writing."

"I'd be so happy, but I dare not read them now," said the cock, "for here comes a hunter—I see him, I see him with his pouch and gun."

When Reynard heard the cock chattering about a hunter, he took to his heels as fast as he could.

BRUIN AND REYNARD PARTNERS

Once on a time Bruin and Reynard owned a field in common. They had a little clearing up in the wood, and the first year they sowed rye.

"Now we must share the crop as is fair and right," said Reynard. "If you like to have the root, I'll take the top."

Yes, Bruin was ready to do that; but when they had threshed out the crop, Reynard got all the corn, but Bruin got nothing but roots and rubbish. He did not like that at all; but Reynard said that was how they had agreed to share it.

"This year I have the gain," said Reynard, "next year it will be your turn. Then you shall have the top, and I shall have to put up with the root."

But when spring came, and it was time to sow, Reynard asked Bruin what he thought of turnips.

"Aye, aye!" said Bruin, "that's better food than rye," and so Reynard thought also. But when harvest time came Reynard got the roots, while Bruin got the turnip-tops. And then Bruin was so angry with Reynard that he put an end at once to his partnership with him.

BOOTS AND HIS BROTHERS

Once on a time there was a man who had three sons, Peter, Paul and Espen. Espen was Boots, of course, because he was the youngest. I can't say the man had anything except these three sons, for he did not possess one penny to rub against another; and so he told his sons over and over again they must go out into the world to seek their fortune, for at home there was nothing to be expected but to starve to death.

Now, a short way from the man's cottage was the King's palace, and you must know, just against the King's windows a great oak had sprung up, which was so stout and big that it took away all the light from the king's palace. The King had said he would give much gold to any man who could fell the oak, but no one was man enough to do it, for as soon as one chip of the oak's trunk flew off, two grew in its stead. The King wished also to have a well dug which was to hold water for the whole year. All his neighbors had wells, but he had none, and he thought that a shame.

So the King said he would give to any one who could dig him such a well as would hold water for the whole year round, both money and goods, but no one could do it, for the King's palace lay high, high up on a hill, and they could dig but a few inches before they would come upon rock.

But as the King had set his heart on having these two things done, he had it given out in all the churches of his kingdom far and wide, that he who could fell the big oak in the King's courtyard, and dig him a well that would hold water the whole year round, should have the Princess and half the kingdom. Well! you may easily know there was many a man who came to try his luck; but all their hacking and hewing, and all their digging and delving were useless. The oak got bigger and stouter at every stroke, and the rock grew no softer either.

One day the three brothers thought they, too, would set off and try it. Their father had not a word to say against it; for even if they did not get the Princess and half the kingdom, it might happen they would get a place somewhere with a good master and that was all he wanted. So when the brothers asked his permission, he consented at once, and Peter, Paul and Espen set forth.

Well, they had not gone far before they came to a fir wood where at one side there rose a steep hill, and as they went along they heard something hewing and hacking away up on the hill among the trees.

"I wonder now what it is that is hewing away up yonder," said Boots.

"You're always so clever with your wondering," laughed Peter and Paul both at once. "What wonder is it, pray, that a wood cutter should stand and hack up on a hillside?"

"Still, I'd like to see what it is, after all," said Boots, and up he went.

"Oh, if you're such a child, 'twill do you good to go and take a lesson," called out his brothers after him.

But Boots didn't care for what they said; he climbed the steep hillside towards the spot whence the noise came, and when he reached the place, what do you think he saw? Why, an axe that stood there hacking and hewing, all of itself, at the trunk of a fir tree.

"Good-day," said Boots. "So you stand here all alone and hew, do you?"

"Yes, here I've stood and hewed and hacked for hundreds of years, waiting for you," said the axe.

"Well, here I am at last," said Boots, as he took the axe, pulled it off its haft, and stuffed both head and haft into his wallet.

When he got down again to his brothers, they began to jeer and laugh at him.

"And now, what strange thing was it you saw up yonder on the hillside?" they asked.

"Oh, it was only an axe we heard," said Boots.

When they had gone on a bit farther, their road passed under a steep spur of rock, where they heard something digging and shovelling.

"I wonder now," said Boots, "what is digging and shovelling up yonder at the top of the rock."

"Ah, you're always so clever with your wondering," laughed Peter and Paul again, "as if you'd never heard a woodpecker hacking and pecking at a hollow tree."

"Well, well," said Boots, "I just think it would be fun to see what it really is."

And so off he set to climb the rock, while the others laughed and made fun of him. But he did not care a bit for that; up he climbed, and when he got near the top, what do you think he saw? Why, a spade that stood there digging and delving.

"Good-day!" said Boots. "So you stand here all alone, and dig and delve, do you?"

"Yes, that's what I do," said the spade, "and that's what I've done these hundreds of years, waiting for you, Boots."

"Well, here I am," said Boots again, as he took the spade and knocked it off the handle, and put it into his wallet,—and then returned to his brothers.

"Well, what was it, so rare and strange," said Peter and Paul, "that you saw up there at the top of the rock?"

"Oh," said Boots, "nothing more than a spade; that was what we heard."

So they went on again a good bit until they came to a brook. They were thirsty, all three, after their long walk, and so they lay down beside the brook to have a drink.

"I wonder now," said Boots, "where all this water comes from."

"I wonder if you've lost the little sense you had," said Peter and Paul in one breath. "Where the brook comes from indeed! Have you never heard how water rises from a spring in the earth?"

"Yes! but still I've a great fancy to see where this brook comes from," said Boots.

So along beside the brook he went, in spite of all that his brothers cried after him. Nothing could stop him. On he went, up and up, and the brook got smaller and smaller, and at last, a little way farther on, what do you think he saw? Why, a great walnut, and out of that the water trickled.

"Good-day!" said Boots again. "So you lie here, and trickle and run down all alone?"

"Yes, I do," said the walnut, "and here have I trickled and run these hundreds of years, waiting for you, Boots."

"Well, here I am," said Boots, as he took up a lump of moss, and plugged up the hole, that the water might not run out. Then he put the walnut into his wallet, and ran down to his brothers.

"Well, now," said Peter and Paul, "have you found out where the water comes from? A rare sight it must have been!"

"Oh, after all, it was only a hole it ran out of," said Boots; and so the others laughed and made fun of him again, but Boots didn't mind that a bit.

"After all, I had the fun of seeing it," said he.

So when they had gone a bit farther, they came to the King's palace; but as every one in the kingdom had heard how he might win the Princess and half the realm, if he could only fell the big oak and dig the King's well, so many had come to try their luck that the oak was now twice as stout and big as it had been at first; for two chips grew for every one they hewed out with their axes, as I dare say you remember I told you. So the King had now laid down as a punishment, that if any one tried and could not fell the oak, he should be put on a barren island, much like a prison.

The two brothers did not let themselves be scared by that, however, for they were quite sure they could fell the oak, and Peter, as he was the eldest, was to try his hand first. But it went with him as with all the rest who had hewn at the oak. For every chip he had cut out, two grew in its place. So the King's men seized him, bound him hand and foot, and put him out on the island.

Now, Paul was to try his luck, but he fared just the same; when he had hewn two or three strokes, they began to see the oak grow, and so the King's men seized him too, bound him hand and foot, and put him out on the island,

And now Boots was to try.

"You can save yourself the trouble, we'll bind you and send you off after your brothers just as well first as last," laughed the King's men.

"Well, I'd just like to try first," said Boots, and so he got leave. Then he took his axe out of his wallet and fitted it to its haft.

"Hew away!" said he to his axe; and away it hewed, making the chips fly, so that it wasn't long before down came the oak.

When that was done Boots pulled out his spade and fitted it to its handle.

"Dig away!" said he to the spade; and the spade began to dig and delve till the earth and rock flew out in splinters, and he had the well soon dug out, as you may believe.

And when he had got it as big and deep as he chose, Boots took out his walnut and laid it in one corner of the well, and pulled the plug of moss out.

"Trickle and run," said Boots; and so the water trickled and ran, till it gushed out of the hole in a stream, and in a short time the well was brimful.

Then Boots had felled the oak which shaded the King's palace, and dug a well that held water all the year around, and so he got the princess and half the kingdom, as the King had said. And it was lucky for Peter and Paul that they were on the barren island, else they had heard each day and hour how every one said: "Well, after all, Boots did not wonder about things for nothing."

THE LAD WHO WENT TO THE NORTH WIND

Once on a time there was an old widow who had one son, and as she was feeble and weak, she asked her son to go out to the storehouse and fetch meal for cooking. But when he got outside the storehouse, and was just going down the steps, there came the North Wind, puffing and blowing, caught up the meal, and away with it through the air. Then the lad went back into the storehouse for more; but when he came out again on the steps, the North Wind came again and carried off the meal with a puff; and more than that, he did it the third time. At this the lad got very angry; and as it seemed hard that the North Wind should behave so, he thought he would go in search of him and ask him to give up his meal.

So off he went, but the way was long, and he walked and walked. At last he came to the North Wind's house.

"Good-day!" said the lad, "and thank you for coming to see us."

"Good-day," answered the North Wind, and his voice was loud and gruff, "and thanks for coming to see me. What do you want?"

"Oh," answered the lad, "I only wished to ask you to be so good as to let me have back the meal you took from me on the storehouse steps, for we haven't much to live on; and if you're to go on snapping up the morsel we have, there'll be nothing for it but to starve."

"I haven't your meal," said the North Wind; "but since you are in such need, I'll give you a table cloth which will get you everything you want. You need only say, 'Cloth, spread yourself, and serve up all kinds of good dishes!'"

With this the lad was well content. But, as the way was long he could not get home in one day, so he turned into an inn on the way; and when they were going to sit down to supper he laid the cloth on the table which stood in the corner, and said,—

"Cloth, spread yourself, and serve up all kinds of good dishes."

He had scarcely said this before the cloth did as it was bid, and all who stood by thought it a fine thing, but most of all the landlord. So, when all were fast asleep, at dead of night, he took the lad's cloth, and put another like it in its stead. But this could not so much as serve up a bit of dry bread.

When the lad woke he took the cloth and went off with it, and that day he got home to his mother.

"Now," said he, "I've been to the North Wind's house, and a good fellow he is, for he gave me this cloth and when I only say to it, 'Cloth, spread yourself, and serve up all kinds of good dishes,' I get every sort of food I please."

"All very true, I dare say," said the mother, "but seeing is believing."

So the lad made haste, drew out a table, laid the cloth on it, and said,—

"Cloth, spread yourself, and serve up all kinds of good dishes."

But not even a bit of dry bread did the cloth serve up.

"Well!" said the lad, "there's no help for it but to go to the North Wind again," and away he went.

So, late in the afternoon, he came to where the North Wind lived.

"Good evening!" said the lad.

"Good evening!" said the North Wind.

"I want my rights for that meal of ours which you took," said the lad, "for, as for that cloth I got, it isn't worth a penny."

"I have no meal," said the North Wind; "but you may have the ram yonder which will coin gold ducats when you say to it,—

"Ram, ram! make money!"

The lad thought this a fine thing; but as it was too far to get home that day, he turned in for the night to the same inn where he had slept the first time.

Before he called for anything, he tried what the North Wind had said of the ram, and found it all true. When the landlord saw this, he thought it a fine ram, and when the lad had fallen asleep, he took another which could not coin even a penny, and exchanged the two.

Next morning off went the lad, and when he got home to his mother, he said,—

"After all, the North Wind is a jolly fellow, for now he has given me a ram, which will coin golden ducats if I only say, 'Ram, ram! make money!'"

"All very true, I dare say," said his mother, "but I shan't believe it until I see the ducats made."

"Ram, ram! make money!" said the lad; but not even a penny did the ram coin.

So the lad went back to the North Wind and scolded him, and said the ram was worth nothing, and he must have his rights for the meal.

"Well!" said the North Wind, "I've nothing else to give you but that old stick in the corner yonder; but it's a stick of such a kind that if you say, 'Stick, stick! lay on! it lays on till you say,—'Stick, stick! now stop!'"

So the lad thanked the North Wind and went his way, and as the road was long, he turned in this night also to the landlord; but as he could guess pretty well how things stood as to the cloth and the ram, he lay down at once on the bench and began to snore, as if he were asleep. Now the landlord who thought surely the stick must be worth something, hunted up one which was like it, and when he heard the lad snore he was going to exchange the two; but, just as the landlord was about to take it, the lad called out,—

"Stick, stick! lay on!"

So the stick began to beat the landlord, till he jumped over chairs and tables and benches, and yelled and roared,—

"Oh my, oh my! bid the stick be still, else it will beat me to death. You shall have back both your cloth and your ram."

When the lad thought the landlord had had enough, he said, "Stick, stick! now stop!"

Then he took the cloth and put it into his pocket, and went home with his stick in his hand, leading the ram by a cord tied around its horns; and so he got his rights for the meal he had lost.

THE GIANT WHO HAD NO HEART IN HIS BODY

Once on a time there was a King who had seven sons. Six of them were stout, brave lads, but the youngest was the cinderlad, you must know; and he went about by himself neither saying nor doing much. Best of all he liked to sit by the hearth and watch the glowing cinders, so they called him Boots, and thought little of him.

Now, when the Princes were grown up, the six were to set off to fetch brides for themselves. As for Boots, they would not be seen with him, so he was to stay at home; but the others were to bring back a bride for him, if any could be found willing to marry such a one. The King gave the six the finest clothes you ever set eyes upon, so fine that the light gleamed from them a long way off; and each had his horse, which cost many, many hundred dollars, and so they set off. Now, when they had been to many palaces, and seen many princesses, they came to a king who had six daughters. Such lovely king's daughters they had never seen, and so they asked them to be their brides, and when they had got them, they set off home again. But they quite forgot that they were to bring back a bride for Boots, their brother, who was staying at home.

When they had gone a good bit on their way, they passed close by a steep hillside, like a wall, where was a giant's house. Out came the giant and set his eyes upon them, and turned them all into stone, princes, princesses and all. Now, the king waited and waited for his six sons, but so long as he waited so long they stayed away; so he fell into great grief, and said he would never know what it was to be happy again.

One day Boots said to the King,—

"I've been thinking to ask your leave to set out and find my brothers."

"Nay, nay!" said his father, "that would be of no use, for you are not clever enough. Better stay and dig in the ashes all your life."

But Boots had set his heart upon it. Go he would; and he begged and pleaded so long that the King was forced to let him go. He gave Boots an old broken-down nag; but Boots did not care a pin for that, he sprang up on his sorry old steed.

"Farewell, Father," he said, "I'll come back, never fear, and likely enough I shall bring my six brothers back with me," and with that he rode off.

When he had ridden a while he came to a raven, which lay in the road and flapped its wings, and was not able to get out of the way, it was so starved.

"Oh, dear friend," said the raven, "give me a little food, and I'll help you again at your utmost need."

"I haven't much food," said the Prince, "and I don't see how you'll ever be able to help me; but still I can spare you a little. I see you need it."

So he gave the raven some of the food he had brought with him.

Now, when he had gone a little farther, he came to a brook, and in the brook lay a great salmon which had got upon a dry place and dashed itself about, and could not get into the water again.

"Oh, dear friend," said the salmon to the Prince; "help me out into the water again, and I'll help you at your utmost need."

"Well!" said the Prince, "the help you'll give me will not be great, I daresay, but it's a pity you should be there and choke;" and with that he shot the fish out into the stream again.

After that he went on a long, long way, and there met him a wolf, which was so famished that it lay and crawled along the road.

"Dear friend, do let me have some food," said the wolf, "I'm so hungry that the wind whistles through my ribs. I've had nothing to eat these two years. When I have eaten, you can ride upon my back, and I'll help you again in your utmost need."

"Well, the help I shall get from you will not be great, I'll be bound," said the Prince; "but you may take all I have, since you are in such great need."

So when the wolf had eaten the food. Boots took the bit and put it between the wolf's jaws, and laid the saddle on his back; and away they went like the wind. Never had the Prince had such a ride before.

"When we have gone still farther," said Graylegs, "I'll show you the Giant's house."

And after a while they came to it.

"See, here is the Giant's house," said the Wolf; "and see, here are your six brothers whom the Giant has turned to stone; and see, here are their six brides. Yonder is the door, and in at that door you must go. When you get in you'll find a princess, and she'll tell you what to do to make an end of the Giant. Only mind you do as she bids you."

Well! Boots went in, but, truth to say, he was very much afraid. The Giant was away, but in one of the rooms sat the Princess, just as the wolf had said, and so lovely a princess Boots had never set eyes upon.

"Oh, heaven help you! whence have you come?" said the Princess, as she saw him; "it will surely be your death. No one can make an end of the Giant who lives here. He is a most cruel monster, and he has no heart in his body."

"Well! well!" said Boots; "but now that I am here, I may as well try what I can do with him, and I will see if I can't free my brothers, who have been turned to stone; and you, too, I will try to save, that I will."

"Well, if you must, you must," said the Princess; "so let us see if we can't hit upon a plan. Just creep under the bed yonder, and mind you listen to what he and I talk about. But, pray, do lie as still as a mouse."

So he crept under the bed, and he had scarce got well underneath, before the Giant came.

"Ha!" roared the Giant, "what a smell of Christian blood there is in the house."

"Yes, I know there is," said the Princess, "for there came a crow flying with a man's bone, and let it fall down the chimney. I made all the haste I could to get it out, but all one can do the smell doesn't go so soon."

So the Giant said no more about it, and when night came they went to bed. After they had lain a while the Princess said, "There is one thing I'd be glad to ask you about, if I only dared."

"What thing is that?" asked the Giant.

"Only this, where do you keep your heart, since you don't carry it about you," said the Princess.

"Ah! that's a thing you've no business to ask about: but if you must know, it lies under the door sill." said the Giant.

"Ho, ho!" said Boots to himself under the bed. "Then we'll soon see if we can't find it."

Next morning the Giant got up very early, and strode off to the wood; but he was hardly out of the house before Boots and the Princess set to work to look under the door sill for this heart; but the more they dug and the more they hunted the more they couldn't find it.

"He has balked us this time," said the Princess, "but we'll try him once more."

So she picked all the prettiest flowers she could find, and strewed them over the door sill, which they had laid in its right place again; and when the time came for the Giant to come home, Boots crept under the bed. Just as he was well under back came the Giant.

Snuff-snuff went the Giant's nose. "My eyes and limbs, what a smell of Christian blood there is in here," said he.

"I know there is," said the Princess, "for there came a crow flying with a man's bone in his bill, and let it fall down the chimney. I made as much haste as I could to get it out, but I dare say it's that you smell."

So the Giant held his peace and said no more about it. A little while after, he asked who it was that had strewed flowers about the door sill.

"Oh, I, of course," said the Princess.

"And, pray, what is the meaning of all this? said the Giant.

"Ah!" said the Princess, "I strewed them there when I knew your heart lay under there."

"You don't say so," said the Giant; "but after all it doesn't lie there at all."

So when they went to bed in the evening, the Princess asked the Giant again where his heart was, for she said she would so much like to know.

"Well," said the Giant, "if you must know, it lies away yonder in the cupboard against the wall."

"So, so!" thought Boots and the Princess; "then we will soon find it."

Next morning the Giant was away early, and strode off to the wood. As soon as he was gone, Boots and the Princess were in the cupboard hunting for the heart, but the more they looked for it the less they found it.

"Well," said the Princess, "we'll just try him once more."

So she decked the cupboard with flowers and garlands, and when the time came for the Giant to come home, Boots crept under the bed again.

Then back came the Giant.

Snuff-snuff! "My eyes and limbs, what a smell of Christian blood there is in here!"

"I know there is," said the Princess, "for a little while since there came a crow flying with a man's bone in his bill, and let it fall down the chimney. I made all the haste I could to get it out of the house; but after all my pains I dare say it's that you smell."

When the Giant heard that he said no more about it, but after a while he saw how the cupboard was all decked about with flowers and garlands; and he asked who it was that had done that. Who could it be but the Princess?

"And, pray what's the meaning of all this foolishness?" asked the Giant.

"Oh, I couldn't help doing it when I knew your heart lay there," said the Princess.

"How can you be so silly as to believe any such thing?" said the Giant.

"How can I help believing it, when you say it?" said the Princess.

"You're a goose," said the Giant; "where my heart is, you will never come."

"Yet for all that," said the Princess, "it would be such a pleasure to know where it really lies."

Then the poor Giant could hold out no longer, but said,—

"Far, far away in a lake lies an island; on that island stands a church; in that church is a well; in that well swims a duck; in that duck there is an egg, and in that egg there lies my heart."

In the morning early, while it was still gray dawn, the Giant strode off to the wood.

"Now I must set off too," said Boots; "if I only knew how to find the way." He took a long farewell of the Princess, and when he slipped out of the Giant's door, there stood the Wolf waiting for him. Boots told him all that had happened, and said now he wished to ride to the well inside the church, if only he knew the way. The Wolf bade him jump on his back, and away they went, over hill and dale, over hedge and field, till the wind whistled after them. After they had travelled many, many days, they came at last to the lake. Then the Prince did not know how to get across, but the Wolf bade him not to be afraid, but to hold fast. So he jumped into the lake with the Prince on his back, and swam over to the island. When they came to the church, the church keys hung high, high up on the top of the tower, and the Prince knew not how to get them down.

"Call upon the raven," said the Wolf.

So the Prince called upon the raven, and immediately the raven came, and flew up and fetched the keys, and so the Prince got into the church. When he came to the well, there was the duck, which swam about forward and backward, just as the Giant had said. So the Prince stood and coaxed it and coaxed it, till finally it came to him, and he grasped it in his hand; but just as he lifted it up from the water the duck dropped the egg in the well, and then Boots was beside himself to know how to get it out again.

"Now call upon the salmon," said the Wolf, and Boots called upon the salmon, and the salmon came and fetched up the egg from the bottom of the well.

Then the Wolf told him to squeeze the egg, and as soon as he squeezed the egg, the Giant screamed and begged and prayed to be spared, saying he would do all that the Prince wished if he would only not squeeze his heart in two.

"Tell him to restore to life again your six brothers and their brides, whom he has turned to stone," said the Wolf. Yes, the Giant was ready to do that, and he turned the six brothers into king's sons again, and their brides into king's daughters.

Then Boots left the Giant's heart on the altar of the church. That took all the evil power from the cruel Giant, and I have never heard of him since.

And now, Boots rode back again on the Wolf to the Giant's house, and there stood all his six brothers alive and merry with their brides. Then Boots went into the hillside after his bride, and they all set off home again to their father's house. And you may fancy how glad the old King was when he saw his seven sons come back, each with his bride;—"But the loveliest bride is the bride of Boots, after all," said the King, "and he shall sit highest at the table, with her by his side."

So they had a great wedding feast, and the mirth was both loud and long, and if they have not done feasting, why they are at it still.

THE SHEEP AND THE PIG WHO SET UP HOUSEKEEPING

Once on a time there was a sheep who stood in the pen to be fattened.

So he lived well and was stuffed and crammed with everything that was good, till one day the dairymaid came to give him still more food. Then she said, "Eat away, sheep, you won't be here much longer, we are going to kill you to-morrow."

The sheep thought over this for a while, and then he ate till he was ready to burst; and when he was crammed full, he butted out the door of the pen, and took his way to the neighboring farm. There he went to see a pig whom he had known out on the common, and with whom he had always been very friendly.

"Good-day," said the sheep, "do you know why it is you are so well off, and why it is they fatten you and take such pains with you?"

"No, I don't," said the pig.

"Well, I know; they are going to kill and eat you," said the sheep.

"Are they?" said the pig, "and what is there to be done about it?"

"If you will do as I do," said the sheep, "we'll go off to the wood, build us a house, and set up for ourselves."

Yes, the pig was willing enough. "Good company is such a comfort," he said, and so the two set off.

When they had gone a bit they met a goose.

"Good-day, good sirs, and whither away so fast to-day?" said the goose.

"Good-day, good-day," said the sheep, "we are going to set up for ourselves in the wood, for you know every man's house is his castle."

"Well," said the goose, "I should so much like a home of my own, too. May I go with you?"

"With gossip and gabble is built neither house nor stable," said the pig, "let us know what you can do."

"I can pluck moss and stuff it into the seams between the planks, and the house will be tight and warm."

Yes, they would give him leave, for, above all things, piggy wished to be warm and comfortable.

So, when they had gone a bit farther—the goose had hard work to walk so fast—they met a hare, who came frisking out of the wood.

"Good-day, good sirs," she said, "how far are you trotting to-day?"

"Good-day, good-day," said the sheep, "we're going to the wood to build us a house and set up for ourselves, for, you know, try all the world around, there's nothing like home."

"As for that," said the hare, "I have a house in every bush, but yet, I have often said in winter, 'If I only live till summer I'll build me a house,' and so I have half a mind to go with you and build one, after all."

"Yes," said the pig, "if we ever get into trouble we might use you to scare away the dogs, for I don't fancy you could help us in house-building."

"Don't make fun of me. I have teeth to gnaw pegs and paws to drive them into the wall, so I can very well set up to be carpenter," said the hare.

So he too got leave to go with them and help to build their house, and there was nothing more to be said about it.

When they had gone a bit farther they met a cock.

"Good-day, good sirs," said the cock, "whither are you going to-day, gentlemen?"

"Good-day, good-day," said the sheep, "we are going off to the wood to build a house and set up for ourselves, for you know, "Tis good to travel east and west, but after all a home is best."'

"Well," said the cock, "if I might have leave to join such a gallant company, I also would like to go to the wood and build a house."

"Ay, ay!" said the pig, "but how can you help us build a house?"

"Oh," said the cock, "what would you do without a cock? I am up early, and I wake every one."

"Very true," said the pig, "let him come with us. Sleep is the biggest thief," he said, "he thinks nothing of stealing half one's life."

So they all set off to the wood together, and built a house.

The pig hewed the timber, and the sheep drew it home; the hare was carpenter, and gnawed pegs and bolts and hammered them into the walls and roof; the goose plucked moss and stuffed it into the seams; the cock crew, and looked out that they did not oversleep themselves in the morning; and when the house was ready, and the roof lined with birch bark and thatched with turf, there they lived by themselves and were merry and well.

But you must know that a bit farther on in the wood was a wolf's den, and there lived two graylegs. When they saw that a new house had been built near by, they wanted to become acquainted with their neighbors. One of them made up an errand and went into the new house and asked for a light for his pipe. But as soon as he got inside the door the sheep gave him such a butt that he fell head foremost into the hearth. Then the pig began to bite him, and the goose to nip and peck him, and the cock upon the roost to crow and chatter, and as for the hare, he was so frightened that he ran about aloft and on the floor and scratched and scrambled in every corner of the house.

So after a time the wolf came out.

"Well," said the one who waited for him outside, "you must have been well received since you stayed so long. But what became of the light? You have neither pipe nor smoke."

"Yes, yes," said the other, "a pleasant company indeed. As soon as I got inside the door, the shoemaker began to beat me with his last, so that I fell head foremost into the open fire, and there sat two smiths who blew the bellows, and made the sparks fly, and struck and punched me with red-hot tongs and pincers. As for the hunter, he went scrambling about looking for his gun, and it was good luck he did not find it. And all the while there was another who sat up under the roof and slapped his arms and cried out, 'Drag him hither, drag him hither!' That was what he screamed, and if he had only got hold of me, I should never have come out alive."

The wolves never went calling on their neighbors any more.

THE PARSON AND THE CLERK

There was once a parson who was such a bully that whenever he met anyone driving on the king's highway, he called out, ever so far off—"Out of the way! Out of the way! Here comes the parson!"

One day when he was driving along and behaving so, he met the king. "Out of the way! Out of the way!" he bawled a long way off. But the king drove on and held his own; so it was the parson who had to turn his horse aside that time, and when the king came up beside him, he said, "To-morrow you shall come to me at the palace, and if you can't answer three questions which I shall ask you, you shall lose your office for your pride's sake."

This was something quite different from what the parson was wont to hear. He could bawl and bully, shout and scold. All that he could do, but question and answer were not in his line. So he set off to the clerk, who was said to be worth more than the parson, and told him he had no mind to go to the king. "For one fool can ask more than ten wise men can answer;" and the end was, he got the clerk to go in his place.

Yes, the clerk set off and came to the palace in the parson's clothes. There the king met him out on the porch with crown and sceptre, and he was so grand he fairly glittered and gleamed. "Well, are you there?" said the king.

"Tell me first," said the king, "how far the east is from the west?"

"Just a day's journey," said the clerk.

"How is that?" asked the king.

"Don't you know," said the clerk, "that the sun rises in the east and sets in the west, and he does it just nicely in a day?"

"Very well!" said the king, "but tell me now what you think I am worth, as you see me stand here?"

"Well," said the clerk, "our Lord was valued at thirty pieces of silver, so I don't think I can set your price higher than twenty-nine."

"All very fine!" said the king, "but, as you are so wise, perhaps you can tell me what I am thinking about now?"

"Oh!" said the clerk, "you are thinking it's the parson who stands before you, but there's where you are mistaken, for I am the clerk."

"Be off home with you," said the king, "and be you parson, and let him be clerk." And so it was.

FATHER BRUIN

Once on a time there was a man who lived far, far away in the wood. He had many, many goats and sheep, but never a one could he keep because of Greylegs, the wolf.

At last he said, "I'll soon trap Greyboots," and so he set to work to dig a pitfall. When he had dug it deep enough, he put a pole down in the midst of the pit, and on the top of the pole he set a board, and on the board he put a little dog. Over the pit itself he spread boughs and branches and leaves, and other rubbish, and a-top of all he strewed snow, so that Greylegs might not see that there was a pit underneath.

So when night came on, the little dog grew weary of sitting there: "Bow-wow, bow-wow," he said, and bayed at the moon. Just then up came a fox, prowling and sneaking, and thought here was a fine time for marketing, and with that gave a jump,—head over heels down into the pitfall.

And when it got a little farther on in the night, the little dog grew so weary and so hungry, and it fell to yelping and howling: "Bow-wow, bow-wow," he cried out. Just at that very moment up came Greylegs, trotting and trotting. He, too, thought he should get a fat steak, and he, too, made a spring—head over heels down into the pitfall.

When it was getting on towards grey dawn in the morning, down fell the snow, with a north wind, and it grew so cold that the little dog stood and shivered and shook, he was so weary and hungry, "Bow-wow, bow-wow, bow-wow," he called out, and barked and yelped and howled. Then up came a bear, tramping and tramping along, and thought to himself how he could get a morsel for breakfast at the very top of the morning, and so he thought and thought among the boughs and branches, till he, too, went bump—head over heels down into the pitfall.

So when it got a little farther on in the morning, an old beggar wife came walking by, who toddled from farm to farm with a bag on her back. When she set eyes on the little dog that stood there and howled, she could not help going near to look and see if any wild beasts had fallen into the pit during the night. So she crawled up on her knees and peeped down into it.

"Art thou come into the pit at last, Reynard?" she said to the fox, for he was the first she saw; "a very good place, too, for such a hen-roost robber as thou; and thou, too, Grey-paw," she said to the wolf; "many a goat and sheep hast thou torn and rent, and now thou shalt be plagued and punished to death. Bless my heart! Thou, too, Bruin! Art thou, too, sitting in this room, thou horse killer? Thee, too, will we strip, and thee shall we flay, and thy skull shall be nailed up on the wall." All this the old lass screeched out as she bent over towards the bear. But just then her bag fell over her ears and dragged her down, and slap! down went the old woman—head over heels into the pitfall.

So there they all four sat and glared at one another, each in a corner—Reynard in one, Greylegs in another, Bruin in a third, and the old woman in a fourth.

But as soon as it was broad daylight, Reynard began to peep and peer, and to twist and turn about, for he thought he might as well try to get out.

But the old lass cried out, "Canst thou not sit still, thou whirligig thief, and not go twisting and turning? Only look at Father Bruin himself in the corner, how he sits as grave as a judge," for now she thought she might as well make friends with the bear.

But just then up came the man who owned the pitfall.

First he drew up the old woman, and after that he slew all the beasts, and neither spared Father Bruin himself in the corner, nor Grey-legs, nor Reynard the whirligig thief. That night, at least, he thought he had made a good haul.

THE PANCAKE

Once on a time there was a woman who had seven hungry children, and she was frying a pancake for them. It was a sweet milk pancake, and there it lay in the pan, bubbling and frizzling so thick and good, it was a delight to look at it. And the children stood round about, and the old father sat by and looked on.

"Oh, give me a bit of pancake, mother, dear, I am so hungry," said one child.

"Oh, darling mother," said the second.

"Oh, darling, good mother," said the third.

"Oh, darling, good, sweet mother," said the fourth.

"Oh, darling, pretty, good, sweet mother," said the fifth.

"Oh, darling, pretty, good, sweet, clever mother," said the sixth.

"Oh, darling, pretty, good, sweet, clever, kindest little mother," said the seventh.

So they begged for the pancake all around, the one more prettily than the other, for they were so hungry and so good.

"Yes, yes, children, only bide a bit till it turns itself"—she ought to have said, 'till I can get it turned,'—"and then you shall have some lovely sweet milk pancake. Only look how fat and happy it lies there."

When the pancake heard all this it became afraid, and in a trice it turned itself and tried to jump out of the pan, but it fell back into it again, the other side up. When it had been fried a little on the other side too, till it got firm and stiff, it jumped out of the pan to the floor and rolled off like a wheel through the door and down the hill.

"Holloa! Stop, pancake!" and away ran the mother after it, with the frying pan in one hand and the ladle in the other, as fast as she could, and all the children behind her, while the old father on crutches limped after them last of all.

"Hi! Won't you stop? Catch it! Stop, pancake!" they all screamed out, one after another, and tried to catch it on the run and hold it. But the pancake rolled on and on, and in a twinkling of an eye it was so far ahead that they couldn't see it.

So when it had rolled awhile it met a man.

"Good-day, pancake," said the man.

"Good-day, Manny Panny!" said the pancake.

"Dear pancake," said the man, "don't roll so fast; stop a little and let me eat you."

"No, no; I have run away from the mother, and the father, and seven hungry children. I'll run away from you, Manny Panny," said the pancake, and it rolled and rolled till it met a hen.

"Good-day, pancake," said the hen.

"The same to you, Henny Penny," said the pancake.

"Pancake, dear, don't roll so fast. Bide a bit and let me eat you up," said the hen.

"No, no; I have run away from the mother, and the father, and seven hungry children, and Manny Panny. I'll run away from you, too, Henny Penny," said the pancake, and it rolled on like a wheel down the road.

Just then it met a cock.

"Good-day, pancake," said the cock.

"The same to you, Cocky Locky," said the pancake.

"Pancake, dear, don't roll so fast, but bide a bit and let me eat you up."

"No, no; I have run away from the mother, and the father, seven hungry children, Manny Panny, and Henny Penny. I'll run away from you too, Cocky Locky," said the pancake, and it rolled and rolled as fast as it could. Bye and bye it met a duck.

"Good-day, pancake," said the duck.

"The same to you, Ducky Lucky."

"Pancake, dear, don't roll away so fast; bide a bit and let me eat you up."

"No, no; I have run away from the mother, and the father, and seven hungry children, Manny Panny, Henny Penny, and Cocky Locky. I'll run away from you, too, Ducky Lucky," said the pancake, and with that it took to rolling and rolling faster than ever; and when it had rolled a long, long while, it met a goose.

"Good-day, pancake," said the goose.

"The same to you, Goosey Poosey."

"Pancake, dear, don't roll so fast; bide a bit and let me eat you up."

"No, no; I have run away from the mother, the father, seven hungry children, Manny Panny, Henny Penny, Cocky Locky, and Ducky Lucky. I'll run away from you, too, Goosey Poosey," said the pancake, and off it rolled.

So when it had rolled a long way off, it met a gander.

"Good-day, pancake," said the gander.

"The same to you, Gander Pander," said the pancake.

"Pancake, dear, don't roll so fast; bide a bit and let me have a bite."

"No, no; I've run away from the mother, the father, seven hungry children, Manny Panny, Henny Penny, Cocky Locky, Ducky Lucky, and Goosey Poosey. I'll run away from you, too, Gander Pander," said the pancake, and it rolled and rolled as fast as ever.

So when it had rolled a long, long time, it met a pig.

"Good-day, pancake," said the pig.

"The same to you, Piggy Wiggy," said the pancake, and without a word more it began to roll and roll for dear life.

"Nay, nay," said the pig, "you needn't be in such a hurry; we two can go side by side through the wood; they say it is not too safe in there."

The pancake thought there might be something in that, and so they kept company. But when they had gone a while, they came to a brook. As for Piggy, he was so fat he could swim across. It was nothing for him, but the poor pancake could not get over.

"Seat yourself on my snout," said the pig, "and I'll carry you over."

So the pancake did that.

"Ouf, ouf," said the pig, and swallowed the pancake at one gulp, and then, as the poor pancake could go no farther, why—this story can go no farther either.

WHY THE SEA IS SALT

Once on a time, but it was a long, long time ago, there were two brothers, one rich and one poor.

Now, one Christmas eve, the poor one had not so much as a crumb in the house, either of meat or bread, so he went to his brother to ask him for something with which to keep Christmas. It was not the first time his brother had been forced to help him, and, as he was always stingy, he was not very glad to see him this time, but he said, "I'll give you a whole piece of bacon, two loaves of bread, and candles into the bargain, if you'll never bother me again—but mind you don't set foot in my house from this day on."

The poor brother said he wouldn't, thanked his brother for the help he had given him, and started on his way home.

He hadn't gone far before he met an old, old man with a white beard, who looked so thin and worn and hungry that it was pitiful to see him.

"In heaven's name give a poor man a morsel to eat," said the old man.

"Now, indeed, I have been begging myself," said the poor brother, "but I'm not so poor that I can't give you something on the blessed Christmas eve." And with that he handed the old man a candle, a loaf of bread, and he was just going to cut off a slice of bacon, when the old man stopped him—"That is enough and to spare," said he. "And now, I'll tell you something. Not far from here is the entrance to the home of the underground folks. They have a mill there which can grind out anything they wish for except bacon; now mind you go there. When you get inside they will all want to buy your bacon, but don't sell it unless you get in return the mill which stands behind the door. When you come out I'll teach you how to handle the mill."

So the man with the bacon thanked the other for his good advice and followed the directions which the old man had given him, and soon he stood outside the door of the hillfolk's home.

When he got in, everything went just as the old man had said. All the hillfolk, great and small, came swarming up to him, like ants around an ant-hill, and each tried to outbid the other for the bacon.

"Well!" said the man, "by rights, my old dame and I ought to have this bacon for our Christmas dinner; but, since you have all set your hearts on it, I suppose I must give it up to you. Now, if I sell it at all, I'll have for it that mill behind the door yonder."

At first the hillfolk wouldn't hear of such a bargain and higgled and haggled with the man, but he stuck to what he said, and at last they gave up the mill for the bacon.

When the man got out of the cave and into the woods again, he met the same old beggar and asked him how to handle the mill. After he had learned how to use it, he thanked the old man and went off home as fast as he could; but still the clock had struck twelve on Christmas eve before he reached his own door.

"Wherever in the world have you been?" said his old dame. "Here have I sat hour after hour, waiting and watching, without so much as two sticks to lay together under the Christmas porridge."

"Oh!" said the man, "I could not get back before, for I had to go a long way first for one thing and then for another; but now you shall see what you shall see."

So he put the mill on the table, and bade it first of all grind lights, then a tablecloth, then meat, then ale, and so on till they had everything that was nice for Christmas fare. He had only to speak the word and the mill ground out whatever he wanted. The old dame stood by blessing her stars, and kept on asking where he had got this wonderful mill, but he wouldn't tell her.

"It's all the same where I got it. You see the mill is a good one, and the mill stream never freezes. That's enough."

So he ground meat and drink and all good things to last out the whole of Christmas holidays, and on the third day he asked all his friends and kin to his house and gave them a great feast. Now, when his rich brother saw all that was on the table and all that was in the cupboards, he grew quite wild with anger, for he could not bear that his brother should have anything.

"'Twas only on Christmas eve," he said to the rest, "he was so poorly off that he came and begged for a morsel of food, and now he gives a feast as if he were count or a king." and he turned to his brother and said, "But where in the world did you get all this wealth?"

"From behind the door," answered the owner of the mill, for he did not care to tell his brother much about it. But later in the evening, when he had gotten a little too merry, he could keep his secret no longer, and he brought out the mill and said:

"There you see what has gotten me all this wealth," and so he made the mill grind all kinds of things.

When his brother saw it, he set his heart on having the mill, and, after some talk, it was agreed that the rich brother was to get it at hay-harvest time, when he was to pay three hundred dollars for it. Now, you may fancy the mill did not grow rusty for want of work, for while he had it the poor brother made it grind meat and drink that would last for years. When hay-harvest came, the rich brother got it, but he was in such a hurry to make it grind that he forgot to learn how to handle it.

It was evening when the rich brother got the mill home, and next morning he told his wife to go out into the hayfield and toss hay while the mowers cut the grass, and he would stay at home and get the dinner ready. So, when dinner time drew near, he put the mill on the kitchen table and said:

"Grind herrings and broth, and grind them good and fast."

And the mill began to grind herrings and broth; first of all the dishes full, then all the tubs full, and so on till the kitchen floor was quite covered. The man twisted and twirled at the mill to get it to stop, but for all his fiddling and fumbling the mill went on grinding, and in a little while the broth rose so high that the man was nearly drowning. So he threw open the kitchen door and ran into the parlor, but it was not long before the mill had ground the parlor full too, and it was only at the risk of his life that the man could get hold of the latch of the house door through the stream of broth. When he got the door open, he ran out and set off down the road, with the stream of herrings and broth at his heels, roaring like a waterfall over the whole farm.

Now, his old dame, who was in the field tossing hay, thought it a long time to dinner, and at last she said:

"Well! though the master doesn't call us home, we may as well go. Maybe he finds it hard work to boil the broth, and will be glad of my help."

The men were willing enough, so they sauntered homewards. But just as they had got a little way up the hill, what should they meet but herrings and broth, all running and dashing and splashing together in a stream, and the master himself running before them for his life, and as he passed them he called out: "Eat, drink! eat, drink! but take care you're not drowned in the broth."

Away he ran as fast as his legs would carry him to his brother's house, and begged him in heaven's name to take back the mill, and that at once, for, said he, "If it grinds only one hour more, the whole parish will be swallowed up by herrings and broth."

So the poor brother took back the mill, and it wasn't long before it stopped grinding herrings and broth.

And now he set up a farmhouse far finer than the one in which his brother lived, and with the mill he ground so much gold that he covered it with plates of gold. And, as the farm lay by the seaside, the golden house gleamed and glistened far away over the sea. All who sailed by put ashore to see the rich man in the golden house, and to see the wonderful mill the fame of which spread far and wide, till there was nobody who hadn't heard of it.

So one day there came a skipper who wanted to see the mill, and the first thing he asked was if it could grind salt.

"Grind salt!" said the owner, "I should just think it could. It can grind anything."

When the skipper heard that, he said he must have the mill, for if he only had it, he thought, he need not take his long voyages across stormy seas for a lading of salt. He much preferred sitting at home with a pipe and a glass. Well, the man let him have it, but the skipper was in such a hurry to get away with it that he had no time to ask how to handle the mill. He got on board his ship as fast as he could and set sail. When he had sailed a good way off, he brought the mill on deck and said, "Grind salt, and grind both good and fast."

And the mill began to grind salt so that it poured out like water, and when the skipper had got the ship full he wished to stop the mill, but whichever way he turned it, and however much he tried, it did no good; the mill kept on grinding, and the heap of salt grew higher and higher, and at last down sank the ship.

There lies the mill at the bottom of the sea, and grinds away to this very day, and that is the reason why the sea is salt—so some folks say.

THE SQUIRE'S BRIDE

There was once a very rich squire who owned a large farm, had plenty of silver at the bottom of his chest, and money in the bank besides; but there was something he had not, and that was a wife.

One day a neighbor's daughter was working for him in the hayfield. The squire liked her very much and, as she was a poor man's daughter, he thought that if he only mentioned marriage she would be more than glad to take him at once. So he said to her, "I've been thinking I want to marry."

"Well, one may think of many things," said the lassie, as she stood there and smiled slyly. She really thought the old fellow ought to be thinking of something that behooved him better than getting married at his time of life.

"Now, you see," he said, "I was thinking that you should be my wife!"

"No, thank you," said she, "and much obliged for the honor."

The squire was not used to being gainsaid, and the more she refused him the more he wanted her. But the lassie would not listen to him at all. So the old man sent for her father and told him that, if he could talk his daughter over and arrange the whole matter for him, he would forgive him the money he had lent him, and would give him the piece of land which lay close to his meadow into the bargain.

"Yes, yes, be sure I'll bring the lass to her senses," said the father. "She is only a child and does not know what is best for her."

But all his coaxing, all his threats and all his talking, went for naught. She would not have the old miser, if he sat buried in gold up to his ears, she said.

The squire waited and waited, but at last he got angry and told the father that he had to settle the matter at once if he expected him to stand by his bargain, for now he would wait no longer.

The man knew no other way out of it, but to let the squire get everything ready for the wedding; then, when the parson and the wedding guests had arrived, the squire would send for the lassie as if she were wanted for some work on the farm. When she got there they would marry her right away, in such a hurry that she would have no time to think it over.

When the guests had arrived the squire called one of his farm lads, told him to run down to his neighbor and ask him to send up immediately what he had promised.

"But if you are not back with her in a twinkling," he said, shaking his fist at him, "I'll——"

He did not finish, for the lad ran off as if he had been shot at.

"My master has sent me to ask for that which you promised him," said the lad, when he got to the neighbor, "but, pray, lose no time, for master is terribly busy to-day."

"Yes, yes! Run down in the meadow and take her with you—there she goes," answered the neighbor.

The lad ran off and when he came to the meadow he found the daughter there raking the hay.

"I am to fetch what your father has promised my master," said the lad.

"Ah, ha!" thought she, "is that what they are up to?" And with a wicked twinkle of the eye, she said, "Oh, yes, it's that little bay mare of ours, I suppose. You had better go and take her. She stands tethered on the other side of the pea field."

The boy jumped on the back of the bay mare and rode home at full gallop.

"Have you got her with you?" asked the squire.

"She is down at the door," said the lad.

"Take her up to the room my mother had," said the squire.

"But, master, how can I?" said the lad.

"Do as I tell you," said the squire. "And if you can't manage her alone, get the men to help you," for he thought the lassie might be stubborn.

When the lad saw his master's face he knew it would be no use to argue. So he went and got all the farm hands together to help him. Some pulled at the head and the forelegs of the mare and others pushed from behind, and at last they got her upstairs and into the room. There lay all the wedding finery ready.

"Well, that's done, master!" said the lad, while he wiped his wet brow, "but it was the worst job I have ever had here on the farm."

"Never mind, never mind, you shall not have done it for nothing," said his master, and he pulled a bright silver coin out of his pocket and gave it to the lad. "Now send the women up to dress her."

"But, I say—master!—"

"None of your talk!" cried the squire. "Tell them to hold her while they dress her, and mind not to forget either wreath or crown."

The lad ran into the kitchen:

"Listen, here, lasses," he called out, "you are to go upstairs and dress up the bay mare as a bride—I suppose master wants to play a joke on his guests."

The women laughed and laughed, but ran upstairs and dressed the bay mare in everything that was there. And then the lad went and told his master that now she was all ready, with wreath and crown and all.

"Very well, bring her down. I will receive her at the door myself," said the squire.

There was a clatter and a thumping on the stairs, for that bride, you know, had no silken slippers on.

When the door was opened and the squire's bride entered the room, you can imagine there was laughing and tittering and grinning enough.

And as for the squire, they say he never went courting again.

42

PEIK

Once on a time there was a man, and he had a wife. They had a son and a daughter who were twins, and these were so alike that no one could tell one from the other except by their clothing. The boy they called Peik. He was of little use while his father and mother lived, for he cared to do naught else than to befool folk, and he was so full of tricks and pranks that no one was left in peace. When the parents died, matters grew still worse and worse. He would not turn his hand to anything. All he would do was to squander what they left behind them.

His sister toiled and moiled all she could, but it helped little; so at last she told him how silly it was to do naught for the house.

"What shall we have to live on when you have wasted everything?" she said.

"Oh, I'll go out and befool somebody," said Peik.

"Yes, Peik, I'll be bound you'll do that soon enough," said the sister.

"Well, I'll try," said Peik.

At last they had indeed nothing more. There was an end of everything; and Peik started off, and walked and walked till he came to the King's palace.

Now, I must tell you, this King and his queen and eldest daughter were little better than trolls,—mean and hateful and very foolish,—so there was no love lost between them and the people.

When Peik came to the King's palace, there stood the King in the porch, and as soon as he set eyes on the lad he said,

"Whither away, to-day, Peik?"

"Oh, I was going out to see if I could befool anybody," said Peik.

"Can't you befool me now?" said the King.

"No, I'm sure I can't," said Peik, "for I've forgotten my fooling rods."

"Can't you go home and fetch them?" said the King, "I should be very glad to see if you are such a trickster as folks say."

"I've no strength to walk," said Peik.

"I'll lend you a horse and saddle," said the King

"But I can't ride either," said Peik.

"We'll lift you up," said the King, "then you'll be able to stick on."

Well, Peik stood and scratched his head as though he would pull the hair off, and he let them lift him up into the saddle. There he sat, swinging this side and that, so long as the King could see him, and the King laughed till the tears came into his eyes, for such a tailor on horseback he had never seen. But when Peik was come well into the wood behind the hill, so that he was out of the King's sight, he sat as though he were tied to the horse, and off he rode as fast as the horse could carry him. But when he got to the town he sold both horse and saddle.

All the while the King walked up and down, and loitered, and waited for Peik to come tottering back again with his fooling rods. And every now and then he laughed when he called to mind how wretched the lad looked as he sat swinging about on the horse like a sack of corn, not knowing on which side to fall off. This lasted for seven lengths and seven breaths, but no Peik came, and so at last the King saw that he was fooled and cheated out of his horse and saddle, even though Peik had not had his fooling rods with him. Then there was another story, for the King got wroth, and was all for setting off to kill Peik.

But Peik had found out the day he was coming, and told his sister she must put on the big boiling-pot with a little water in it. Just as the King came in, Peik dragged the pot off the fire and ran off with it to the chopping-block, and so boiled the porridge on the block.

The King wondered at that, and wondered on and on, so much that he quite forgot what brought him there.

"What do you want for that pot?" said he.

"I can't spare it," said Peik.

"Why not?" said the King; "I'll pay what you ask."

"No, no!" said Peik. "It saves me time and money, wood hire and chopping hire, carting and carrying."

"Never mind," said the King, "I'll give you a hundred dollars. It's true you've fooled me out of a horse and saddle, and bridle besides, but all that shall go for nothing if I can only get the pot."

"Well, if you must have it, you must," said Peik.

When the King got home he asked guests and made a feast, but the meat was to be boiled in the new pot, and so he took it up and set it in the middle of the floor. The guests thought the King had lost his wits, and went about elbowing one another, and laughing at him. But he walked round and round the pot and cackled and chattered, saying all in a breath—

"Well, well! bide a bit, bide a bit! 'Twill boil in a minute."

But there was no boiling. So he saw that Peik had been out with his fooling rods and had cheated him again, and now he would set off at once and slay him.

When the King came, Peik stood out by the barn door. "Wouldn't it boil?" he asked.

"No, it would not, and you shall smart for it," said the King, about to unsheath his knife.

"I can well believe that," said Peik, "for you did not take the block, too."

"I wish I thought," said the King, "you weren't telling me a pack of lies."

"I tell you it's because of the block it stands on; it won't boil without it," said Peik.

"Well, what do you want for it?"

It was well worth three hundred dollars; but for the King's sake it should go for two. So the King got the block and traveled home with it. He bade guests again, made a feast, and set the pot on the chopping-block in the middle of the room. The guests thought he was both daft and mad, and they went about making game of him, while he cackled and chattered around the pot, calling out, "Bide a bit! Now it boils, now it boils in a trice."

But it wouldn't boil a bit more on the block than on the bare floor. So he saw that Peik had been out with his fooling rods this time, too. Then he fell a-tearing his hair, and said he would set off at once and slay the lad. He wouldn't spare him this time, whether or no.

But Peik was ready for him. He had filled a leather bag with blood and stuffed it into his sister's bosom, and told her what to say and do.

"Where's Peik?" screamed out the King. He was in such a rage that he stuttered and stammered.

"He is so poorly that he can't stir hand or foot," she said, "and now he's trying to get a nap."

"Wake him up!" said the King.

"Nay, I daren't, he will be so angry," said the sister.

"Well, I am angrier still," said the King, "and if you don't wake him, I will," and with that he tapped his side where his knife hung.

"Well, she would go and wake him," but Peik turned hastily in his bed, drew out a knife and ripped open the leather bag in her bosom, so that the blood gushed out, and down she fell on the floor as though she were dead.

"What an awful fellow you are, Peik," said the King; "you have killed your sister right before my eyes!"

"Oh, there's no trouble with her so long as there's breath in my nostrils," said Peik, and with that he pulled out a ram's horn and began to toot on it.

"Toot-e-too-too," he blew, with one end of the horn to her body, and up she rose as though there was nothing the matter with her.

"Dear me, Peik! Can you kill folk and blow life into them again? Can you do that?" said the King.

"Why!" said Peik, "how could I get on at all if I couldn't? I am always killing every one I come near; don't you know I have a terrible temper?"

"I am hot-tempered, too," said the King, "and that horn I must have. I'll give you a hundred dollars for it, and besides I'll forgive you for cheating me out of my horse and for fooling me about the pot and the block, and all else."

Peik was loth to part with it, but for his sake he would let him have it. And so the King went off home with it, and he hardly got back before he must try it.

So he fell a-wrangling and quarreling with the queen and his eldest daughter, and they paid him back in the same coin; but before they knew what was happening he had whipped out his knife and cut their throats. They fell down stone dead and the other two daughters ran from the house, they were so afraid.

The King walked about the floor for a while and kept chattering that there was no harm done so long as there was breath in him, and then he pulled out the horn and began to blow "Toot-e-too-too! Toot-e-too-too!" but, though he blew and tooted as hard as he could all that day and the next, too, he could not blow life into them again. Dead they were, and dead they stayed. But the people in the kingdom were only glad to get rid of such troll-folk, and were wishing some one might make an end of the King, too, so that they might have a good King in his place.

But the King was now angrier than ever, and must go right off to kill Peik.

But Peik knew that he was coming and then he said to his sister—

"Now, you must change clothes with me and set off. If you will do that, you may have all we own."

So, she changed clothes with him, packed up and started off as fast as she could; but Peik sat all alone in his sister's clothes.

"Where is that Peik?" roared the King, as as he came, in a towering rage, through the door.

"He has run away," said Peik. "He knew that your Majesty was coming, so he left me all alone without a morsel of bread or a penny in my purse," and he made himself as gentle and sweet as a young lady.

"Come along, then, to the King's palace, and you shall have enough to live on. There's no good sitting here and starving in this cabin by yourself," said the King.

So Peik went home with the King, and there he was treated as the King's own daughter, for Miss Peik sewed and stitched and sang and played with the others, and was with them early and late.

But one day a man came to the King and told him that Peik's sister was at a farm in the neighborhood, and that it was Peik he had brought up in his own house. Now, Peik had heard all that the man told the King, so he ran away from the King's palace, out into the wide world.

The King got into a terrible rage then, and called for Peik, but he was nowhere to be found. Then he mounted his horse to go out to look for Peik.

He had not gone far before he came to a ploughed field and there sat Peik on a stone, playing on a mouth organ.

"What! Are you sitting there, Peik?" said the King.

"Here I sit, sure enough," said Peik; "where else should I sit?"

"You have cheated me foully time after time," said the King, "but now you must come along home with me, and I'll kill you."

"Well, well," said Peik, "if it can't be helped, it can't; I suppose I must go along with you."

When they got home to the King's palace they got ready a barrel which Peik was to be put in, and when it was ready they carted it up a high mountain. There he was to lie three days, thinking on all the evil he had done, then they were to roll him down the mountain into the sea.

The third day a rich man passed by and when he heard Peik's story he was ready to help him out of his trouble.

They made a stuffed man and put him with some stones into the barrel— but the rich man gave Peik horses and cows, sheep and swine, and money beside.

Now, the King came to roll Peik down the mountain. "A happy journey!" said the King, "and now it is all over with you and your fooling rods."

Before the barrel was halfway down the mountain there was not a whole stave of it left, nor would there have been a whole limb on Peik, had he been there. But when the King came back to the palace, Peik was there before him, and sat in the court-yard playing on his mouth organ.

"What! You sitting here, you, Peik?"

"Yes! Here I sit, sure enough. Where else should I sit?" said Peik. "Maybe I can get room here for all my horses and sheep and money."

"But whither was it that I rolled you that you got all this wealth?" asked the King.

"Oh, you rolled me into the sea," said Peik, "and when I got to the bottom there was more than enough and to spare, both of horses and sheep, and of gold and silver. The cattle went about in great flocks, and the gold and silver lay in large heaps as big as houses."

"What will you take to roll me down the same way?" asked the King.

"Oh," said Peik, "it costs little or nothing to do it. Besides, you took nothing from me, and so I'll take nothing from you either."

So he stuffed the King into a barrel and rolled him over, and when he had given him a ride down to the sea for nothing, he went home to the King's palace.

Then he began to hold his bridal feast with the youngest princess, and afterwards he ruled the land both well and long. But he kept his fooling rods to himself, and kept them so well that nothing was ever heard of Peik and his tricks, but only of "Ourself the King."

THE PRINCESS WHO COULD NOT BE SILENCED

There was once a King, and he had a daughter who was so cross and crooked in her words that no one could silence her, and so he gave it out that he who could do it should marry the princess and have half the kingdom, too. There were plenty of those who wanted to try it, I can tell you, for it is not every day that you can get a princess and half a kingdom. The gate to the King's palace did not stand still a minute. They came in great crowds from the East and the West, both riding and walking. But there was not one of them who could silence the princess.

At last the king had it given out that those who tried, and failed, should have both ears marked with the big redhot iron with which he marked his sheep. He was not going to have all that flurry and worry for nothing.

Well, there were three brothers, who had heard about the princess, and, as they did not fare very well at home, they thought they had better set out to try their luck and see if they could not win the princess and half the kingdom. They were friends and good fellows, all three of them, and they set off together.

When they had walked a bit of the way, Boots picked up something.

"I've found—I've found something!" he cried.

"What did you find!" asked the brothers.

"I found a dead crow," said he.

"Ugh! Throw it away! What would you do with that?" said the brothers, who always thought they knew a great deal.

"Oh, I haven't much to carry, I might as well carry this," said Boots.

So when they had walked on a bit, Boots again picked up something.

"I've found—I've found something!" he cried.

"What have you found now?" said the brothers.

"I found a willow twig," said he.

"Dear, what do you want with that? Throw it away!" said they.

"Oh, I haven't much to carry, I might as well carry that," said Boots.

So when they had walked a bit, Boots picked up something again. "Oh, lads, I've found—I've found something!" he cried.

"Well, well, what did you find this time?" asked the brothers.

"A piece of a broken saucer," said he.

"Oh, what is the use of that? Throw it away!" said they.

"Oh, I haven't much to carry, I might as well carry that," said Boots.

And when they had walked a bit further, Boots stooped down again and picked up something else.

"I've found—I've found something, lads!" he cried.

"And what is it now?" said they.

"Two goat horns," said Boots.

"Oh! Throw them away. What could you do with them?" said they.

"Oh, I haven't much to carry, I might as well carry them," said Boots.

In a little while he found something again.

"Oh, lads, see, I've found—I've found something," he cried.

"Dear, dear, what wonderful things you do find! What is it now?" said the brothers.

"I've found a wedge," said he.

"Oh, throw it away. What do you want with that?" said they.

"Oh, I haven't much to carry, I might as well carry that," said Boots.

And now, as they walked over the fields close up to the King's palace, Boots bent down again and held something in his fingers.

"Oh, lads, lads, see what I've found!" he cried.

"If you only found a little common sense, it would be good for you," said they. "Well, let's see what it is now."

"A worn-out shoe sole," said he.

"Pshaw! Well, that was something to pick up! Throw it away! What do you want with that?" said the brothers.

"Oh, I haven't much to carry, I might as well carry that, if I am to win the princess and half the kingdom," said Boots.

"Yes, you are likely to do that—you," said they.

And now they came to the King's palace. The eldest one went in first.

"Good-day," said he.

"Good-day to you," said the princess, and she twisted and turned.

"It's awfully hot here," said he.

"It is hotter over there in the hearth," said the princess. There lay the red-hot iron ready awaiting. When he saw that he forgot every word he was going to say, and so it was all over with him.

And now came the next oldest one.

"Good-day," said he.

"Good-day to you," said she, and she turned and twisted herself.

"It's awfully hot here," said he.

"It's hotter over there in the hearth," said she. And when he looked at the red-hot iron he, too, couldn't get a word out, and so they marked his ears and sent him home again.

Then it was Boots' turn.

"Good-day," said he.

"Good-day to you," said she, and she twisted and turned again.

"It's nice and warm in here," said Boots.

"It's hotter in the hearth," said she, and she was no sweeter, now the third one had come.

"That's good, I may bake my crow there, then?" asked he.

"I'm afraid she'll burst," said the princess.

"There's no danger; I'll wind this willow twig around," said the lad.

"It's too loose," said she.

"I'll stick this wedge in," said the lad, and took out the wedge.

"The fat will drop off," said the princess.

"I'll hold this under," said the lad, and pulled out the broken bit of the saucer.

"You are crooked in your words, that you are," said the princess.

"No, I'm not crooked, but this is crooked," said the lad, and he showed her the goat's horn.

"Well, I never saw the equal to that!" cried the princess.

"Oh, here is the equal to it," said he, and pulled out the other.

"Now, you think you'll wear out my soul, don't you?" said she.

"No, I won't wear out your soul, for I have a sole that's worn out already," said the lad, and pulled out the shoe sole.

Then the princess hadn't a word to say.

"Now, you're mine," said Boots.

And so she was.

THE TWELVE WILD DUCKS

Once on a time there was a Queen who had twelve sons but no daughter.

One day she was out driving in the woods and met the prettiest little lassie one ever did see, and so the Queen stopped her horses, lifted the child up in her arms, kissed her on both cheeks, all the while thinking:

"I wish I had a little girl of my own, oh, how long I've waited and wished for one."

Just then an old witch of the trolls came up to her, but you wouldn't have known it was a witch at all, she looked so kind and good.

"A daughter you shall have," she said, "and she shall be the prettiest child in twelve kingdoms, if you will give to me what ever comes to meet you at the bridge."

Now the Queen had a little snow white dog of which she was very fond, and it always ran to meet her when she had been away. She thought, of course, it was the dog the old dame wanted, so the Queen said, "Yes, you may have what comes to meet me on the bridge." With that she hurried home as fast as she could.

But, who should come to meet her on the bridge but her twelve sons; and before the mother could cry out to them the wicked witch threw her spell upon them and turned them into twelve ducks which flapped their wings and flew away. Away they went and away they stayed.

But the Queen had a daughter, and she was the loveliest child one ever set eyes upon. The Princess grew up, and she was both tall and fair, but she was often quiet and sorrowful, and no one could understand what it was that ailed her. The Queen, too, was often sorrowful, as you may believe, for she had many strange fears when she thought of her sons. And one day she said to her daughter, "Why are you so sorrowful, lassie mine? Is there anything you want? If so, only say the word, and you shall have it."

"Oh, it seems so dull and lonely here," said the daughter, "every one else has brothers and sisters, but I am all alone; I have none. That's why I'm so sorrowful."

"But you had brothers, my daughter," said the Queen; "I had twelve sons, stout, brave lads, but I lost them all when you came;" and so she told her the whole story.

When the Princess heard that she had no rest; for she thought it was all her fault, and in spite of all the Queen could say or do, though she wept and prayed, the lassie would set off to seek her brothers. On and on she walked into the wide world, so far you would never have thought her small feet could have had strength to carry her so far.

Finally, one day, when she was walking through a great, great wood, she felt tired, and sat down on a mossy tuft and fell asleep. Then she dreamt that she went deeper and deeper into the wood, till she came to a little wooden hut, and there she found her brothers. Just then she awoke, and straight before her she saw a worn path in the green moss. This path went deeper into the wood, so she followed it, and after a long time she came to just such a little wooden house as that she had seen in her dream.

Now, when she went into the room there was no one at home, but there were twelve beds, and twelve chairs, and twelve spoons,—in short, a dozen of everything. When she saw that she was very glad; she had not been so glad for many a long year, for she could guess at once that her brothers lived there, and that they owned the beds and chairs and spoons. So she began to make up the fire, and sweep the room and make the beds and cook the dinner, and to make the house as tidy as she could.

And when she had done all the work and the dinner was on the table she suddenly heard something flapping and whirling in the air, and she slipped behind the door. Then all the twelve ducks came sweeping in; but as soon as ever they crossed the threshold they became Princes.

"Oh, how nice and warm it is here," they said, "Heaven bless him who made up the fire and cooked such a nice dinner for us."

"But who can it be?" said the youngest Prince, and they all hunted both high and low until they found the lassie behind the door. And she threw her arms around their necks and said, "I'm your sister; I've gone about seeking you these three years, and if I could set you free, I'd willingly give my life."

Then all the brothers looked sorrowfully, one at the other, and they shook their heads.

"No, it's too hard," said the eldest Prince, looking at the pretty young Princess, "it's too hard," and again they sighed and shook their heads.

"Oh, tell me, only tell me," said the Princess, "how can it be done, and I'll do it, whatever it be." And as she begged and pleaded for them to tell her, the youngest brother said at last, "You must pick thistledown, and you must card it, and spin it, and weave it. After you have done that, you must cut out and make twelve shirts, one for each of us, and while you do that, you must neither talk, nor laugh, nor weep. If you can do that we are free."

"But where shall I ever get thistledown enough for so many shirts?" asked the sister.

"Well, that is the hardest thing of all," said the eldest brother. "You must go to the witches' moor at midnight and gather it there," and big tears stood in his eyes, "and you must go alone, all alone."

But the sister smiled and nodded her head, and when midnight came, and the moon was high in the sky she said good-bye to her brothers, and went to the great, wide moor, where the witches lived. There stood a great crop of thistles, all nodding and nodding in the breeze, while the down floated and glistened like gossamer through the air in the moonbeams. The Princess began to pluck and gather it as fast as she could, but she saw long skinny arms outstretched toward her, and, among the thistles, she saw a host of wicked faces all looking at her. Her heart stood still then and she grew icy cold, but never a sound did she utter, only plucked and gathered until her bag was full; and when she got home at break of day she set to work carding and spinning yarn from the down.

So she went on a long, long time picking down on the witches' moor, carding and spinning, and all the while keeping the house of the Princes, cooking, and making their beds. But she never talked, nor laughed, nor wept.

At evening home the brothers came, flapping and whirring like wild ducks, and all night they were Princes, but in the morning off they flew again, and were wild ducks the whole day.

But, it happened one night when she was out on the moor picking thistledown, that the young King who ruled that land was out hunting, and had lost his way. He had become separated from his companions, and now, as he came riding across the moor, he saw her. He stopped and wondered who the lovely lady could be that walked alone on the moor picking thistledown in the dead of the night; and he asked her name. Getting no answer, he was still more astonished, but he liked her so much, that at last nothing would do but he must take her home to his castle and marry her. So he took her and put her upon his horse. The Princess wrung her hands, and made signs to him, and pointed to the bags in which her work was, and when the King saw she wished to have them with her he took the bags and placed them behind them.

When that was done the Princess, little by little, came to herself, for the King was both a wise man and a handsome man, and he was as gentle and kind to her as a mother. But when they reached the palace an old woman met them. She was the King's guardian, and when she set eyes on the Princess she became so cross and jealous of her, because she was so lovely, that she said to the King:

"Can't you see now, that this thing whom you have picked up, and whom you are going to marry, is a witch? Why, she can neither talk nor laugh nor weep!"

But the King did not care a straw for what she said. He held to the wedding and married the Princess, and they lived in great joy and glory. But the Princess didn't forget to go on working on her shirts, and she neither talked nor laughed nor wept. However, when she had spun and woven and cut, she found that she still had not enough cloth for the twelve shirts, and she needs must go to the witches' moor again.

So that night while all the palace slept she quietly slipped out and walked off to pick her thistledown, but the old woman who was the King's guardian saw her, and she knew well where the young Queen was going, for I must tell you she was the same wicked witch who had changed the twelve Princes into wild ducks. She hurried to the King's chamber, woke him and said, "Now, come with me and I'll prove to you that your lovely Queen is a witch, who joins the wicked company on the moor at midnight." The King would not listen to her at first, but when he saw that the Queen's bed was empty, he got up and went with the old woman.

And there upon the edge of the moor they stopped, but in the clear moonlight they could see the Queen among the horrid hags and trolls. The King turned away sadly and said not a word, for he loved his quiet Queen very much.

But the wicked old woman began to whisper and tell abroad about the Queen's nightly visit to the moor, and at last the King's best men came to him and said, "We will not have a Queen who is a witch; the people demand of you that she be burnt alive."

Then the King was so sad that there was no end to his sadness, for now he saw that he could not save her. He was obliged to order her to be burnt alive on a pile of wood. When the pile was all ablaze, and they were about to put her on it, she made signs to them to take twelve boards and lay them around the pile.

On these she laid the shirts for her brothers all completed but that for the youngest, which lacked its left sleeve; she had not had time to finish it. And as soon as ever she had done that, they heard a flapping and whirring in the air, and down came twelve wild ducks from over the forest, and each snapped up his shirt in his bill and flew off with it.

"See now!" said the old woman to the King, "wasn't I right when I told you she was a witch! Make haste and burn her before the pile burns low."

"Oh!" said the King, "we've wood enough and to spare, and so I'll wait a bit, for I have a mind to see what the end of this will be."

As he spoke up came the twelve Princes riding along, as handsome well-grown lads as you'd wish to see; but the youngest Prince had a wild duck's wing instead of his left arm. "What's all this about?" asked the Princes.

"My Queen is to be burnt," said the King, "because she is a witch, so the people say, and I can't save her."

"Speak now, sister," said the Princes, "you have set us free and saved us, now save yourself."

Then the young Queen spoke and told the whole story, and the King and all the people listened with wonder and joy. Only the wicked old woman stood trembling with fear. And when the Queen had finished her story, the people took the old witch and bound her and burned her on the pile.

But the King took his wife and the twelve Princes and went home with them to their father and mother, and told all that had befallen them. Then there was joy and gladness over the whole kingdom, because the wicked witch was dead and the Princes saved and set free, and because the lovely Princess had set free her twelve brothers.

GUDBRAND-ON-THE-HILLSIDE

Once upon a time there was a man whose name was Gudbrand. He had a farm which lay far, far away upon a hillside, and so they called him Gudbrand-on-the-Hillside.

Now, you must know this man and his good wife lived so happily together, and understood one another so well, that all the husband did the wife thought so well done there was nothing like it in the world, and she was always pleased at whatever he turned his hand to. The farm was their own land, and they had a hundred dollars lying at the bottom of their chest and two cows tethered up in a stall in their farmyard.

So one day his wife said to Gudbrand, "Do you know, dear, I think we ought to take one of our cows into town and sell it; that's what I think; for then we shall have some money in hand, and such well-to-do people as we ought to have ready money as other folks have. As for the hundred dollars in the chest yonder, we can't make a hole in our savings, and I'm sure I don't know what we want with more than one cow.

"Besides, we shall gain a little in another way, for then I shall get off with only looking after one cow, instead of having, as now, to feed and litter and water two."

Well, Gudbrand thought his wife talked right good sense, so he set off at once with the cow on the way to town to sell her; but when he got to the town, there was no one who would buy his cow.

"Well, well, never mind," said Gudbrand, "at the worst, I can only go back home with my cow. I've both stable and tether for her, and the road is no farther out than in." And with that he began to toddle home with his cow.

But when he had gone a bit of the way, a man met him who had a horse to sell. Gudbrand thought 'twas better to have a horse than a cow, so he traded with the man. A little farther on he met a man walking along and driving a fat pig before him, and he thought it better to have a fat pig than a horse, so he traded with the man. After that he went a little farther, and a man met him with a goat, so he thought it better to have a goat than a pig, and he traded with the man who owned the goat. Then he went on a good bit till he met a man who had a sheep, and he traded with him too, for he thought it always better to have a sheep than a goat. After a while he met a man with a goose, and he traded away the sheep for the goose; and when he had walked a long, long time, he met a man with a cock, and he traded with him, for he thought in this wise, "Tis surely better to have a cock than a goose."

Then he went on till the day was far spent, and he began to get very hungry, so he sold the cock for a shilling, and bought food with the money, for, thought Gudbrand-on-the-Hillside, "Tis always better to save one's life than to have a cock."

After that he went on homeward till he reached his nearest neighbor's house, where he turned in.

"Well," said the owner of the house, "how did things go with you in town?"

"Rather so-so," said Gudbrand, "I can't praise my luck, nor do I blame it either," and with that he told the whole story from first to last.

"Ah!" said his friend, "you'll get nicely hauled over the coals, when you go home to your wife. Heaven help you, I wouldn't stand in your shoes for anything."

"Well," said Gudbrand-on-the-Hillside, "I think things might have gone much worse with me; but now, whether I have done wrong or not, I have so kind a good wife she never has a word to say against anything that I do."

"Oh!" answered his neighbor, "I hear what you say, but I don't believe it for all that."

"And so you doubt it?" asked Gudbrand-on-the-Hillside.

"Yes," said the friend, "I have a hundred crowns, at the bottom of my chest at home, I will give you if you can prove what you say."

So Gudbrand stayed there till evening, when it began to get dark, and then they went together to his house, and the neighbor was to stand outside the door and listen, while the man went in to his wife.

"Good evening!" said Gudbrand-on-the Hillside.

"Good evening!" said the good wife. "Oh! is that you? Now, I am happy."

Then the wife asked how things had gone with him in town.

"Oh, only so-so," answered Gudbrand; "not much to brag of. When I got to town there was no one who would buy the cow, so you must know I traded it away for a horse."

"For a horse," said his wife; "well that is good of you; thanks with all my heart. We are so well to do that we may drive to church, just as well as other people, and if we choose to keep a horse we have a right to get one, I should think." So, turning to her child she said, "Run out, deary, and put up the horse."

"Ah!" said Gudbrand, "but you see I have not the horse after all, for when I got a bit farther on the road, I traded it for a pig."

"Think of that, now!" said the wife. "You did just as I should have done myself; a thousand thanks! Now I can have a bit of bacon in the house to set before people when they come to see me, that I can. What do we want with a horse? People would only say we had got so proud that we couldn't walk to church. Go out, child, and put up the pig in the sty."

"But I have not the pig either," said Gudbrand, "for when I got a little farther on, I traded it for a goat."

"Dear me!" cried the wife, "how well you manage everything! Now I think it over, what should I do with a pig? People would only point at us and say 'Yonder they eat up all they have.' No, now I have a goat, and I shall have milk and cheese, and keep the goat too. Run out, child, and put up the goat."

"Nay, but I haven't the goat either," said Gudbrand, "for a little farther on I traded it away and got a fine sheep instead!"

"You don't say so!" cried his wife, "why, you do everything to please me, just as if I had been with you. What do we want with a goat? If I had it I should lose half my time in climbing up the hills to get it down. No, if I have a sheep, I shall have both wool and clothing, and fresh meat in the house. Run out, child, and put up the sheep."

"But I haven't the sheep any more than the rest," said Gudbrand, "for when I got a bit farther, I traded it away for a goose."

"Thank you, thank you, with all my heart," cried his wife, "what should I do with a sheep? I have no spinning wheel or carding comb, nor should I care to worry myself with cutting, and shaping, and sewing clothes. We can buy clothes now as we have always done; and now I shall have roast goose, which I have longed for so often; and, besides, down with which to stuff my little pillow. Run out, child, and put up the goose.

"Well!" said Gudbrand, "I haven't the goose either; for when I had gone a bit farther I traded it for a cock."

"Dear me!" cried his wife, "how you think of everything! just as I should have done myself. A cock! think of that! Why it's as good as an eight day clock, for every day the cock crows at four o'clock, and we shall be able to stir our stiff legs in good time. What should we do with a goose? I don't know how to cook it; and as for my pillow, I can stuff it with cotton grass. Run out, child, and put up the cock."

"But after all, I haven't the cock either," said Gudbrand, "for when I had gone a bit farther, I became as hungry as a hunter, so I was forced to sell the cock for a shilling, for fear I should starve."

"Now, God be praised that you did so!" cried his wife, "whatever you do, you do it always just after my own heart. What should we do with the cock? We are our own masters, I should think, and can lie abed in the morning as long as we like. Heaven be thanked that I have you safe back again; you who do everything so well, that I want neither cock nor goose; neither pigs nor kine."

Then Gudbrand opened the door and said,—

"Well, what do you say now? Have I won the hundred crowns?" and his neighbor was forced to admit that he had.

THE PRINCESS ON THE GLASS HILL

Once on a time, there was a man who had a meadow, which lay high upon the hillside, and in the meadow was a barn, which he had built to keep his hay in. Now, I must tell you there hadn't been much in the barn for the last year or two, for every St. John's night, when the grass stood greenest and deepest, the meadow was eaten down to the very ground the next morning, just as if a whole drove of sheep had been there feeding on it over night. This happened once, and it happened twice; so at last the man grew weary of losing his crop of hay, and said to his sons—for he had three of them, and the youngest was nicknamed Boots, of course—that now one of them must just go and sleep in the barn in the outlying field when St. John's night came, for it was no joke that his grass should be eaten, root and blade, this year, as it had been the last two years. So whichever of them went must keep a sharp look-out; that was what their father said.

Well, the eldest son was ready to go and watch the meadow; trust him for looking after the grass. So, when evening came, he set off to the barn, and lay down to sleep. But a little on in the night came such a clatter, and such an earthquake, that walls and roof shook, and groaned, and creaked. Then up jumped the lad, and took to his heels as fast as ever he could; nor dared he once look around until he reached home; and as for the hay, why it was eaten up this year just as it had been twice before.

The next St. John's night, the man said again it would never do to lose all the grass in the outlying field year after year in this way, so one of his sons must just trudge off to watch it, and watch it well too. Well, the next oldest son was ready to try his luck, so he set off and sat down to watch in the barn as his brother had done before him. But as the night wore on, there came on a rumbling and quaking of the earth, worse even than on the last St. John's night, and when the lad heard it, he got frightened, and took to his heels as though he were running a race.

Next year the turn came to Boots; but when he made ready to go the other two began to laugh and to make game of him, saying,—

"You're just the man to watch the hay, that you are; you, who have done nothing all your life but sit in the ashes and toast yourself by the fire."

But Boots did not care a pin for their chattering, and as evening drew on, he walked up the hillside to the outlying field. There he went inside the barn and sat down; but in about an hour's time the barn began to groan and creak, so that it was dreadful to hear.

"Well," said Boots to himself, "if it isn't worse than this, I can stand it well enough."

A little while after came another creak and an earthquake, so that the litter in the barn flew about the lad's ears.

"Oh!" said Boots to himself, "if it isn't worse than this, I daresay I can stand it out."

But just then came a third rumbling and a third earthquake, so that the lad thought walls and roof were coming down on his head; but it passed off, and all was still as death about him.

"It'll come again, I'll be bound," thought Boots; but no, it didn't come again; still it was, and still it stayed. But after he had sat a little while, he heard a noise as if a horse were standing just outside the barn door, and feeding on the grass. He stole to the door, and peeped through a chink, and there stood a horse feeding away. So big, and fat, and grand a horse, Boots had never set eyes on. By his side on the grass lay a saddle and bridle, and a full set of armor for a knight, all of brass, so bright that the light gleamed from it.

"Ho, ho!" thought the lad; "it's you, is it, that eats up our hay?"

So he lost no time, but took the steel out of his tinder box and threw it over the horse; then it had no power to stir from the spot, and became so tame that the lad could do what he liked with it. Then he got on its back, and rode off with it to a place which no one knew of, and there he put up the horse. When he got home, his brothers laughed, and asked how he had fared.

"You didn't sit long in the barn, even if you had the heart to go as far as the field."

"Well," said Boots, "all I can say is, I sat in the barn till the sun rose."

"A pretty story," said his brothers; "but we'll soon see how you have watched the meadow;" so they set off; but when they reached it, there stood the grass as deep and thick as it had been over night.

Well, the next St. John's eve it was the same story over again; neither of the elder brothers dared to go out to the outlying field to watch the crop; but Boots, he had the heart to go, and everything happened just as it had the year before. First a clatter and an earthquake, then a greater clatter and another earthquake, and so on a third time; only this year the earthquakes were far worse than the year before. Then all at once everything was still as death, and the lad heard how something was cropping the grass outside the barn door, so he stole to the door, and peeped through a chink; and what do you think he saw? Why, another horse standing right up against the wall, and chewing and champing with might and main. It was far larger and finer than that which came the year before, and it had a saddle on its back, and a bridle on its head, and a full suit of mail for a knight lay by its side, all of silver, and as splendid as you would wish to see.

"Ho, ho!" said Boots to himself; "it's you that gobbles up our hay, is it?" And with that he took the steel out of his tinder box, and threw it over the horse's crest; then it stood as still as a lamb. Well, the lad rode this horse, too, to the hiding place where he kept the other one, and after that, he went home.

"I suppose you'll tell us," said one of his brothers, "there's a fine crop this year too, up in the hay field."

"Well, so there is," said Boots; and off ran the others to see, and there stood the grass thick and deep, as it was the year before; but they didn't give Boots softer words for all that.

Now, when the third St. John's eve came, the two elder still hadn't the heart to sit out in the barn and watch the grass, for they had got so scared at heart the night they sat there before, that they couldn't get over the fright. But Boots dared to go; and the very same thing happened this time that had happened twice before. Three earthquakes came, one after the other, each worse than the one which went before, and when the last came, the lad danced about with the shock from one barn wall to the other; and after that, all at once, it was still as death. Now, when he had sat a little while, he heard something cropping away at the grass outside the barn, so he stole again to the door chink, and peeped out, and there stood a horse outside—far, far bigger and more beautiful than the two he had taken before. It had a saddle on its back, a bridle on its head, and a full suit of mail for a knight lay by its side—all of gold, all more splendid than anything you ever saw.

"Ho, ho!" said the lad to himself, "it's you, is it, that comes here eating up our hay? I'll soon stop that." So he caught up his steel, and threw it over the horse's neck, and in a trice it stood as if it were nailed to the ground, and Boots could do as he pleased with it. Then he rode off with it to the hiding place, where he kept the other two, and then went home. When he got home, his two brothers made game of him as they had done before, saying, they could see he had watched the grass well, for he looked for all the world as if he were walking in his sleep, and many other spiteful things they said, but Boots gave no heed to them, only asking them to go and see for themselves; and when they went, there stood the grass as fine and deep this time as it had been twice before.

Now you must know that the king of the country where Boots lived had a daughter, whom he would only give to the man who could ride up over the hill of glass, for there was a high, high hill, all of glass, as smooth and slippery as ice, close by the king's palace. Upon the tip top of the hill the king's daughter was to sit, with three golden apples in her lap, and the man who could ride up and carry off the three golden apples was to have half the kingdom, and the Princess to wife. This offer the king had posted on all the church doors in his realm; and had given it out in many other kingdoms besides. Now, this Princess was so lovely, that all who set eyes on her loved her. So I needn't tell you how all the princes and knights who heard of her were eager to win her to wife, and half the kingdom besides; and how they came riding from all parts of the world on high prancing horses, and clad in the grandest clothes, for there wasn't one of them who hadn't made up his mind that he, and he alone, was to win the Princess.

So when the day of trial came, which the king had fixed, there was such a crowd of princes and knights under the glass hill, that it made one's head whirl to look at them; and every one in the country who could even crawl along was off to the hill, for they all were eager to see the man who was to win the Princess. Thus the two elder brothers set off with the rest; but as for Boots, they said outright he shouldn't go with them, for if they were seen with such a dirty fellow, all begrimed with smut from cleaning their shoes, and sifting cinders in the dust-hole, they said folk would make game of them.

"Very well," said Boots; "it's all one to me. I can go alone."

Now, when the two brothers came to the hill of glass, the knights and princes were all hard at it, riding their horses till they were all in a foam; but it was no good; for as soon as ever the horses set foot on the hill, down they slipped, and there wasn't one who could get a yard or two up; and no wonder, for the hill was as smooth as a sheet of glass, and as steep as a house-wall. But all were eager to have the Princess and half the kingdom. So they rode and slipped, and slipped and rode, and still it was the same story over again. At last all their horses were so weary that they could scarce lift a leg, and so the knights had to give up trying any more.

The king was just thinking that he would proclaim a new trial for the next day, to see if they would have better luck, when all at once a knight came riding up on so brave a steed, that no one had ever seen the like of it in his born days, and the knight had a mail of brass, and the horse a brass bit in his mouth, so bright that the sunbeams shone from it. Then all the others called out to him that he might just as well spare himself the trouble of riding at the hill, for it would lead to no good; but he gave no heed to them, and put his horse at the hill, and went up it for a good way, about a third of the height; and when he had got so far, he turned his horse round and rode down again. So lovely a knight the Princess thought she had never yet seen; and while he was riding, she sat and thought to herself,—

"Ah, how I wish that he might come up and go down the other side."

And when she saw him turning back, she threw down one of the golden apples after him, and it rolled down into his shoe. But when he got to the bottom of the hill he rode off so fast that no one could tell what had become of him. That evening all the knights and princes were to go before the king, that he who had ridden so far up the hill might show the apple which the Princess had thrown, but there was no one who had anything to show. One after the other they all came, but not a man of them could show the apple.

The next day, all the princes and knights began to ride again, and you may fancy they had taken care to shoe their horses well; but it was no use,—they rode and slipped, and slipped and rode, just as they had done the day before; and there was not one who could get so far as a yard up the hill. And when they had worn out their horses, so that they could not stir a leg, they were all forced to give it up. So the king thought he might as well proclaim that the riding should take place the day after for the last time, just to give them one chance more; but all at once it came across his mind that he might as well wait a little longer, to see if the knight in brass mail would come this day too. Well! they saw nothing of him; but all at once came one riding on a steed, far, far braver and finer than that on which the knight in brass had ridden, and he had silver mail, and a silver saddle and bridle, all so bright that the sunbeams gleamed and glanced from them far away. Then the others shouted out to him again, saying he might as well stop, and not try to ride up the hill, for all his trouble would be thrown away. But the knight paid no heed to them, and rode straight at the hill, and right up it, till he had gone two-thirds of the way, and then he wheeled his horse around and rode down again. To tell the truth, the Princess liked him still better than the knight in brass, and she sat and wished he might be able to come right up to the top, and down the other side; but when she saw him turning back, she threw the second apple after him, and it rolled down and fell into his shoe. But as soon as ever he had come down the hill of glass, he rode off so fast that no one could see what became of him.

At even, all were to go in before the king and the Princess, that he who had the golden apple might show it. In they went, one after the other, but there was no one who had any apple to show.

The third day everything happened as it had happened the two days before. There was no one who could get so much as a yard up the hill; and now all waited for the knight in silver mail, but they neither saw nor heard of him. At last came one riding on a steed, so brave that no one had ever seen his match; and the knight had a suit of golden mail, and a golden saddle and bridle, so wondrous bright that the sunbeams gleamed from them a mile off. The other knights and princes could not find time to call out to him not to try his luck, for they were amazed to see how grand he was. So he rode at the hill, and tore up it like nothing, so that the Princess hadn't even time to wish that he might get up the whole way. As soon as ever he reached the top, he took the third golden apple from the Princess's lap, and then turned his horse and rode down again. As soon as he got down he rode off at full speed, and was out of sight in no time.

Now, when the two brothers got home at even, you may fancy what long stories they told, how the riding had gone off that day; and amongst other things, they had a deal to say about the knight in golden mail.

"He just was a chap to ride," they said; "so grand a knight isn't to be found in this wide world."

Next day all the knights and princes were to pass before the king and the Princess—that he who had the gold apple might bring it forth; but one came after another, first the princes, then the knights, and still no one could show the gold apple.

"Well," said the king, "some one must have it, for it was something that we all saw with our own eyes, how a man came and rode up and bore it off."

So he commanded that everyone who was in the kingdom should come up to the palace and see if he could show the apple. Well, they all came one after another, but no one had the golden apple, and after a long time the two brothers of Boots came. They were the last of all, so the king asked them if there was no one else in the kingdom who hadn't come.

"Oh, yes," said they; "we have a brother, but he never carried off the golden apple. He hasn't stirred out of the dust-hole on any of the three days."

"Never mind that," said the king; "he may as well come up to the palace like the rest." So he came.

"How, now," said the king; "have you the golden apple? Speak out."

"Yes, I have," said Boots; "here is the first, and here is the second, and here is the third, too;" and with that he pulled all three golden apples out of his pocket, and at the same time threw off his sooty rags, and stood before them in his gleaming golden mail.

"Yes," said the king; "you shall have my daughter, and half my kingdom, for you well deserve both her and it."

So they got ready for the wedding, and Boots got the Princess to wife, and there was great merry-making at the bridal-feast, you may fancy, for they could all be merry though they couldn't ride up the hill of glass; and all I can say is, if they haven't left off their merry-making yet, why, they're still at it.

THE HUSBAND WHO WAS TO MIND THE HOUSE

Once on a time there was a man so mean and cross that he never thought his wife did anything right in the house. So one evening in hay-making time he came home scolding and tearing, and showing his teeth and making a fuss.

"Dear love, don't be so angry; there's a good man," said his goody; "to-morrow let's change our work. I'll go out with the mowers and mow, and you shall mind the house at home."

The husband thought that would do very well. He was quite willing, he said.

So, early next morning his goody took a scythe on her shoulders, and went out into the hayfield with the mowers, and began to mow; but the man was to mind the house and do the work at home.

First of all he wanted to churn the butter; but when he had churned a while, he grew thirsty and went down to the cellar to tap a barrel of ale. So, just when he was putting the tap into the cask, he heard overhead the pig come into the kitchen. Then off he ran up the cellar steps, with the tap in his hand, as fast as he could to look after the pig, lest it should upset the churn. But when he got up, and saw the pig had already knocked the churn over and stood there grunting and rooting in the cream which was running all over the floor, he became so wild with rage, that he quite forgot the ale barrel, and ran at the pig as hard as he could.

He caught it, too, just as it ran out of doors, and gave it such a kick that piggy died on the spot. Then all at once he remembered he had the tap in his hand; but when he got down to the cellar, every drop of ale had run out of the cask.

Then he went into the dairy and found enough cream left to fill the churn again, and so he began to churn, for butter they must have at dinner. When he had churned a bit, he remembered that their milking cow was still shut up in its stall, and had not had a mouthful to eat or a drop to drink all the morning, though the sun was high. Then he thought it was too far to take her down to the meadow, so he'd just get her up on the house top, for the house, you must know, was thatched with sods, and a fine crop of grass was growing there. Now their house lay close up against a steep rock, and he thought if he laid a plank across to the roof at the back, he'd easily get the cow up.

But still he could not leave the churn, for there was their little babe crawling about the floor, and, "If I leave it," he thought, "the child is sure to upset it."

So he took the churn on his back and went out with it. Then he thought he'd better water the cow before he turned her out on the thatch, and he took up a bucket to draw water out of the well. But, as he stooped down at the brink of the well, all the cream ran out of the churn over his shoulders, about his neck, and down into the well.

Now it was near dinner time, and he had not even got butter yet. So he thought he'd best boil the porridge, and he filled the pot with water, and hung it over the fire. When he had done that, he thought the cow might perhaps fall off the thatch and break her legs or her neck. So he got up on the house to tie her up. One end of the rope he made fast to the cow's neck, and the other he slipped down the chimney and tied round his own waist. He had to make haste, for the water now began to boil in the pot, and he had still to grind the oatmeal.

So he began to grind away; but while he was hard at it, down fell the cow off the housetop after all, and as she fell she dragged the man up the chimney by the rope. There he stuck fast. And as for the cow, she hung halfway down the wall, swinging between heaven and earth, for she could neither get down nor up.

And now the goody had waited seven lengths and seven breadths for her husband to come and call them home to dinner, but never a call they had. At last she thought she'd waited long enough and went home.

When she got there and saw the cow hanging in such an ugly place, she ran up and cut the rope in two with her scythe. But as she did this, down came her husband out of the chimney, and so when his old dame came inside the kitchen, there she found him standing on his head in the porridge pot.

LITTLE FREDDY WITH HIS FIDDLE

Once there was a farmer who had an only son. The lad had had very poor health so he could not go out to work in the field.

His name was Freddy, but, since he remained such a wee bit of a fellow, they called him Little Freddy. At home there was but little to eat and nothing at all to burn, so his father went about the country trying to get the boy a place as cowherd or errand boy; but there was no one who would take the weakly little lad till they came to the sheriff. He was ready to take him, for he had just sent off his errand boy, and there was no one who would fill his place, for everybody knew the sheriff was a great miser.

But the farmer thought it was better there than nowhere; he would get his food, for all the pay he was to get was his board—there was nothing said about wages or clothes. When the lad had served three years he wanted to leave, and the sheriff gave him all his wages at one time. He was to have a penny a year. "It couldn't well be less," said the sheriff. And so he got three pence in all.

As for Little Freddy, he thought it was a great sum, for he had never owned so much; but, for all that, he asked if he wasn't to have anything for clothes, for those he had on were worn to rags. He had not had any new ones since he came to the sheriff's three years ago.

"You have what we agreed on," said the sheriff, "and three whole pennies besides. I have nothing more to do with you. Be off!"

So Little Freddy went into the kitchen and got a little food in his knapsack, and after that he set off on the road to buy himself more clothes. He was both merry and glad, for he had never seen a penny before, and every now and then he felt in his pockets as he went along to see if he had them all three. So, when he had gone far and farther than far, he got up on top of the mountains. He was not strong on his legs, and had to rest every now and then, and then he counted and counted how many pennies he had. And now he came to a great plain overgrown with moss. There he sat down and began to see if his money was all right. Suddenly a beggarman appeared before him, so tall and big that when he got a good look at him and saw his height and length, the lad began to scream and screech.

"Don't you be afraid," said the beggarman, "I'll do you no harm, I came only to beg you for a penny."

"Dear me!" said the lad, "I have only three pennies, and with them I was going to town to buy clothes."

"It is worse for me than for you," said the beggarman, "I have not one penny, and I am still more ragged than you."

"Well, that is so; you shall have it," said the lad.

When he had walked on a while, he grew weary again, and sat down to rest. Suddenly another beggarman stood before him, and this one was still taller and uglier than the first. When the lad saw how very tall and ugly and long he was, he began to scream again.

"Now, don't you be afraid of me," said the beggar, "I'll do you no harm. I came only to beg for a penny."

"Oh dear, oh dear!" said the lad. "I have only two pennies, and with them I was going to the town to buy clothes. If I had only met you sooner, then—"

"It's worse for me than for you," said the beggarman. "I have no penny, and a bigger body and less clothing."

"Well, you may have it," said the lad. So he went away farther, till he got weary, and then he sat down to rest; but he had scarcely sat down when a third beggarman came to him. This one was so tall and ugly and long that the lad had to look up and up, right up to the sky. And when he took him all in with his eyes, and saw how very, very tall and ugly and ragged he was, he fell a-screeching and screaming again.

"Now, don't you be afraid of me, my lad," said the beggarman, "I'll do you no harm, for I am only a beggarman, who begs you for a penny."

"Oh dear, oh dear!" said the lad. "I have only one penny left, and with it I was going to the town to buy clothes. If I had only met you sooner, then—"

"As for that," said the beggarman, "I have no penny at all, that I haven't, and a bigger body and less clothes, so it is worse for me than for you."

"Yes," said Little Freddy, "he must have the penny then—there was no help for it; for so each beggarman would have one penny, and he would have nothing."

"Well," said the beggarman, "since you have such a good heart that you gave away all that you had in the world, I will give you a wish for each penny." For you must know it was the same beggarman who had got them all three; he had only changed his shape each time, that the lad might not know him again.

"I have always had such a longing to hear a fiddle go, and see folk so merry and glad that they couldn't help dancing," said the lad; "and so if I may wish what I choose, I will wish myself such a fiddle, that everything that has life must dance to its tune."

"That you may have," said the beggarman, "but it is a sorry wish. You must wish something better for the other two pennies."

"I have always had such a love for hunting and shooting," said Little Freddy; "so if I may wish what I choose, I will wish myself such a gun that I shall hit everything I aim at, were it ever so far off."

"That you may have," said the beggarman, "but it is a sorry wish too. You must wish better for the last penny."

"I have always had a longing to be in company with folks who were kind and good," said Little Freddy; "and so, if I could get what I wish, I would wish it to be so that no one can say 'Nay' to the first thing I ask."

"That wish is not so sorry," said the beggarman; and off he strode between the hills, and Freddy saw him no more.

So the lad lay down to sleep, and the next day he came down from the mountain with his fiddle and his gun. First he went to the storekeeper and asked for clothes. Next at a farm he asked for a horse, and at a second for a sleigh; and at another place he asked for a fur coat. No one said him "Nay"—even the stingiest folk were all forced to give him what he asked for. At last he went through the country as a fine gentleman, and had his horse and his sleigh. When he had gone a bit he met the sheriff whose servant he had been.

"Good day, master," said Little Freddy, as he pulled up and took off his hat.

"Good day," said the sheriff, "but when was I ever your master?"

"Oh yes," said Little Freddy, "don't you remember how I served you three years for three pence?"

"My goodness, now!" said the sheriff, "you have grown rich in a hurry, and pray, how was it that you got to be such a fine gentleman?"

"Oh, that is a long story," said Little Freddy.

"And are you so full of fun that you carry a fiddle about with you?" asked the sheriff.

"Yes, yes," said Freddy. "I have always had such a longing to get folk to dance. But the funniest thing of all is this gun, for it brings down almost anything that I aim at, however far it may be off. Do you see that magpie yonder, sitting in the spruce fir? What will you give me if I hit it as we stand here?"

"Well," said the sheriff, and he laughed when he said it, "I'll give you all the money I have in my pocket, and I'll go and fetch it when it falls," for he never thought it possible for any gun to carry so far.

But as the gun went off down fell the magpie, and into a great bramble thicket; and away went the sheriff up into the bramble after it, and he picked it up and held it up high for the lad to see. But just then Little Freddy began to play his fiddle, and the sheriff began to dance, and the thorns to tear him; but still the lad played on, and the sheriff danced, and cried, and begged, till his clothes flew to tatters, and he scarce had a thread to his back.

"Yes," said Little Freddy, "now I think you're about as ragged as I was when I left your service; so now you may get off with what you have."

But first the sheriff had to pay him all the money that he had in his pocket.

So when the lad came to town he turned into an inn, and there he began to play, and all who came danced and laughed and were merry, and so the lad lived without any care, for all the folks liked him and no one would say "Nay" to anything he asked.

But one evening just as they were all in the midst of their fun, up came the watchmen to drag the lad off to the town hall; for the sheriff had laid a charge against him, and said he had waylaid him and robbed him and nearly taken his life. And now he was to be hanged. The people would hear of nothing else. But Little Freddy had a cure for all trouble, and that was his fiddle. He began to play on it, and the watchmen fell a-dancing and they danced and they laughed till they gasped for breath.

So soldiers and the guard were sent to take him, but it was no better with them than with the watchmen. When Little Freddy played his fiddle, they were all bound to dance; and dance as long as he could lift a finger to play a tune; but they were half dead long before he was tired.

At last they stole a march on him, and took him while he lay asleep by night. Now that they had caught him they could condemn him to be hanged on the spot, and away they hurried him to the gallows tree.

There a great crowd of people flocked together to see this wonder, and the sheriff too was there. He was glad to get even at last for the money and the clothes he had lost, and to see the lad hanged with his own eyes.

And here came Little Freddy, carrying his fiddle and his gun. Slowly he mounted the steps of the gallows,—and when he got to the top he sat down, and asked if they could deny him a wish, and if he might have leave to do one thing? He had such a longing, he said, to scrape a tune and play a bar on his fiddle before they hanged him.

"No, no," they said; "it were sin and shame to deny him that." For you know, no one could say "Nay" to what he asked.

But the sheriff begged them not to let him have leave to touch a string, else it would be all over with them altogether. If the lad leave, he begged them to bind him to the birch that stood there.

Little Freddy was not slow in getting his fiddle to speak, and all that were there fell a-dancing at once, those who went on two legs, and those who went on four. Both the dean and the parson, the lawyer and the sheriff, masters and men, dogs and pigs—they all danced and laughed and barked and squealed at one another. Some danced till they lay down and gasped, some danced till they fell in a swoon. It went badly with all of them, but worst of all with the sheriff; for there he stood bound to the birch, and he danced till he scraped the clothes off his back. I dare say it was a sorry looking sight and a sore back.

But there was not one of them who thought of doing anything to Little Freddy, and away he went with his fiddle and his gun, whither he chose, and he lived merrily and happily all his days, for there was no one who could say "Nay" to the first thing he asked for.

Echo Library
www.echo-library.com

Echo Library uses advanced digital print-on-demand technology to build and preserve an exciting world class collection of rare and out-of-print books, making them readily available for everyone to enjoy.

Situated just yards from Teddington Lock on the River Thames, Echo Library was founded in 2005 by Tom Cherrington, a specialist dealer in rare and antiquarian books with a passion for literature.

Please visit our website for a complete catalogue of our books, which includes foreign language titles.

The Right to Read

Echo Library actively supports the Royal National Institute for the Blind's Right to Read initiative by publishing a comprehensive range of Large Print (16 point Tiresias font as recommended by the RNIB) and Clear Print (13 point Tiresias font) titles for those who find standard print difficult to read.

Customer Service

If there is a serious error in the text or layout please send details to feedback@echo-library.com and we will supply a corrected copy. If there is a printing fault or the book is damaged please refer to your supplier.

Printed in the United States
86786LV00005B/232/A